BREAKING HER NO-DATING RULE

BY
AMALIE BERLIN

First published in Great Britain 2015
by Mills & Boon, an imprint of Harlequin (UK) Limited,
Large Print edition 2015
Eton House, 18-24 Paradise Road,
Richmond, Surrey, TW9 1SR

© 2015 Amalie Berlin

ISBN: 978-0-263-25487-7

Printed and bound in Great Britain
by CPI Antony Rowe, Chippenham, Wiltshire

There's never been a day when there haven't been stories in **Amalie Berlin**'s head. When she was a child they were called daydreams, and she was supposed to stop having them and pay attention. Now when someone interrupts her daydreams to ask, 'What are you doing?' she delights in answering, 'I'm working!'

Amalie lives in Southern Ohio with her family and a passel of critters. When *not* working, she reads, watches movies, geeks out over documentaries and randomly decides to learn antiquated skills. In case of zombie apocalypse she'll still have bread, lacy underthings, granulated sugar, and always something new to read.

Recent titles by Amalie Berlin:

RETURN OF DR IRRESISTIBLE
UNCOVERING HER SECRETS
CRAVING HER ROUGH DIAMOND DOC

These books are also available in eBook format from www.millsandboon.co.uk

PROLOGUE

"I KNOW THAT you want to manage this situation yourself, but you do have to relax at some point. Let me and the universe carry the load for a few days."

The fact that most of the resort had been abandoned at the first hint of the approaching storm gave Ellory Star more confidence than she might've otherwise had in what would be an intense situation at best. Only a handful of staff remained—enough to keep the resort running—and a handful of guests trying to get in as much time on the powder as they could before the clouds rolled in. But it wasn't like Mira was leaving the premises. She'd be around for catastrophe, her safety net.

"Enjoy your post-coital vacation, spend time with Mr. Forever, Number Five. I promise not to refer to him any more in any way that highlights the fact that I totally won the New Year's resolution war this year." Ellory leaned over the bar in Jack's suite, where she and Mira were chatting, tidied a stack of napkins emblazoned with the lodge logo, and pretended not to be feeling smug about how totally right she was.

Mira—her sister by everything except genetics and actual family ties—was the concierge doctor for the ski lodge where Ellory was now living and working, and her best friend since they'd set eyes on one another as toddlers, when Ellory's mother had brought her to work at the lodge Mira's family owned. She was the brilliant one, and rational, dependable, smart, and a lot of other good-sounding words that everybody would use to describe Mira and only Mira would ever use to label her.

"You haven't won until you figure out your quest. Your project. The thing you're working on."

A project Ellory hadn't explained. "I should've just bet you I could go without a man longer than you could keep serial dating. Though I haven't seen any contenders for sexy fun since I've been home. So the resolution is safe."

But that wouldn't have served the point of her making the resolution to begin with. Besides, her inability to articulate exactly what was wrong was part of the problem she needed to figure out. She skated through life, largely flying on instinct and ignoring anything that hurt her to the point that she wasn't even sure what hurt her any more. For the past year she'd been running from some pain she couldn't name—because ignoring the reasons for pain didn't mean she didn't feel it. It just meant she felt it blindly.

Her quest had led her home, and left her with the understanding that she had something to work on. Banishing men from her life kept her from sublimating with sex, kept her from distracting herself. She'd spent a decade distracting herself with a string of different boyfriends, and she wasn't any closer to finding enlightenment…or just plain old happiness…than she had been when she'd left home, determined to give her life meaning.

Before things got too deep, before Mira picked up on the melancholy lurking in Ellory's soul, she shifted the subject back to one she knew Mira couldn't resist. "So, I'm going to have to come up with a new nickname for Jack. I could make some 'playing doctor' references, but that's too obvious."

Jack's timely arrival through the suite door was her cue. "Hey, *Loooove* Doctor," she called, and then shook her head. "Nah, that's not it. I'll keep working on it. Somewhere else now that we've got everything hashed out." She winked at Mira and brushed past Mr. Mira on the way to the door.

Before she stepped out she turned to say something, and interrupted kissing. "Man, I was going to say that I was totally wrong about the resolution—that it just wasn't that Jack was lucky to be the fifth dude but that I believed he was the one...and would have been if he'd been number twenty-five or number five. Now I just want to give you a safe-sex talk!"

When they both laughed at her she smiled and cooed at them both while closing the door, "Oh, Number Five, you'll always be number *one* to me!"

The door clicked before she could get pelted with bar paraphernalia for her pretend Mira-sex-talk.

The universe did like her. Occasionally.

CHAPTER ONE

ELLORY STAR HAD never been a sentinel before, and there were good reasons for that.

But this was where her mission to find herself had led. From the hot, life-laden forests of Peru to Colorado in the winter. To cold legs and a head full of static, hair that stuck to everything, and, of course, to trying to find other people. Correction, she wasn't even out doing the heavy lifting on the finding. She was just waiting for other people to find people.

The universe had a wicked sense of humor.

A tight cluster of yellow headlights flickered in the far left of her field of vision and soon grew strong enough to cut through the gray-blue haze of hard-falling snow.

The rescue team was back!

She turned from the frosty glass inset in the polished brass doors of the Silver Pass Lodge to face the ragtag group of employees she'd managed to round up after the mass exodus. Most lodge employees had families they wanted to get to before the blizzard hit, and nearly all the patrons had left too—the ones who hadn't left were the ones the rescue team was returning with. She hoped.

"Okay, guys, do the things we talked about," she said—the most order-like order she'd ever given.

Usually, she was the last person to be put in charge of anything, and that was how Ellory liked it. She had less chance of letting people down if they didn't expect anything from her. It probably highlighted some flaw in her character that the only time she was willing to take on any kind of serious responsibility was when her primary objective was guarding her best friend's sexy rendezvous time.

Ellory—gatekeeper to the love shack.

She who kept non-emergency situations from disturbing the resort doctor while she got her wild thing on with Jack, aka Number Five.

Pure. Accomplishment.

She watched long enough to see the first staff member break into motion, placing another log on the already blazing fire and opening the damper so the lobby fireplace would roar to life.

Later she could feel guilty for the amount of carbon she was responsible for putting into the atmosphere today. Right now, her heart couldn't find a balance between the well-being of people around her and the well-being of the planet.

Some lifestyle choices were harder to live with than others.

Those returning would be cold at the very least, and Ellory prayed that was the worst of their afflictions. Cold she could remedy with fire, hot beverages, hot water, and blankets hot from the clothes dryer—even if all those warm things further widened her expanding carbon footprint and left her feeling like a sasquatch. A big, hypocritical, sooty-footed, carbon-belching sasquatch.

And those kinds of thoughts were not helping. She had no room for negativity today. She had a job, she had a plan, she'd see it through and not let anyone down—especially the only one with any faith in her.

One of them should be having wild monkey sex with someone, and as she wasn't having any she'd defend Mira's love shack to the last possible minute. Be the stand-in Mira today, and do the very best she could for as long as she could. At least until she knew exactly what Mira would have to deal with when it got to be too much for *her* to handle.

When she looked back at the headlights, they'd grown close enough for her to count. Six sets, same number as had gone out. Good sign.

She fastened the coat she wore, crammed a knit cap on her head and pushed her hands into her mittens. Her clothes might be ridiculous since she hadn't yet augmented her wardrobe with Colorado winter wear, and her bottom half might freeze when she went out to meet the team, but at least the places where she kept her important bits—organs, brain—would be warm.

As the snowmobiles rolled to a stop in front of the ornate doors, she took a last deep breath of warm air and pushed out into the raging winter. Wind whipped her gauzy, free-flowing skirt around her legs and made it hard to keep her eyes open. With one hand shielding them from the blast of snowy, frigid air, she counted: ten people, one dog.

Should have been eleven.

Another quick count confirmed that all the six rescuers in orange had made it back, which meant one of the lodge's patrons was still lost in this storm that was forecast to only get worse.

Oh, no.

She'd have to disturb Mira.

People were already climbing off the snowmobiles, rescuers in their orange suits helping more fashionably dressed and slower-moving guests from the machines.

"How can I help?" she called over the wind, approaching the group.

The large man paused in his task of releasing a big snowy black dog from the cage on the back of his snowmobile, turned and pointed at Ellory. *"Get inside now!"*

Real yelling? Okay… Maybe it was just to get over the wind.

He unlatched the cage and his canine friend bounded out. The sugar-frosted dog didn't need to be told where to go. Ellory made it to the outer doors behind the massive canine and opened it for him, then held it for people.

It wasn't technically a blizzard yet. It was snowing hard, yes, and blowing harder, and of course she was cold, but she wouldn't freeze to death in the next couple of minutes while she helped in some fashion. And she needed to help. Even if all she could think to do was hold the door.

As the man approached, he lifted his goggles and sent a baleful stare at her, stormier than the weather. With one smooth motion he grabbed Ellory's elbow and thrust her ahead of him into the breezeway, "That wasn't a suggestion. Get inside now. You're not dressed for the weather."

"I didn't offer to make snow angels with anyone," she joked, looking over her shoulder at the angry man as he steered her inside.

Stumbling, she pulled her elbow free and pushed through, intent on getting some space between them.

Good grief. Up close, and without fabric covering the bottom of his face or the goggles concealing his eyes, the fact that he was working some kind of rugged handsome look canceled the effect of winter and made her feel like she was dipped in peppermint wherever she touched him.

Ellory didn't get those kind of excited feelings for anyone ever, not without really working at it. Must be the cold. And now that she was inside, she had things to do besides tingle and lust after Ole Yeller.

A specific list of things, in fact, to look for when checking these people out.

As the group gathered around the fireplace and the hats and goggles came off, she got a good look at how beaten down they all were. Exhausted. Weak. All of them, both the rescuers and the rescued. But those who didn't do this for a living, the ones who'd been helpless and still had a missing friend, looked blank. It was the same shell-shocked expression she'd seen on the faces of victims of natural disasters—earthquakes, mudslides, and floods. Being lost in a snowstorm probably counted...

Her people stood around, waiting for her. Follower to leader for one day—no wonder they didn't know what to do. She was supposed to be leading them. Her list of things had *hypothermia* at the very top as the most important situation to remedy.

"Okay, guys, we need to help everyone get out of their snow suits and boots. Get the hot blankets on them. And hot beverages. Hot cocoa..." she corrected. Everyone liked cocoa, and it was loaded with calories they no doubt needed after their harrowing day.

While the employees did as she asked, Ellory backtracked to the Angry Dog Man. He seemed much more leader-like than she felt, so he got the questions.

In hushed tones, she asked, "Where is the other one?"

He frowned, his left hand lifting to his right shoulder to grip and squeeze through the thick coat he wore. "The other one tried to get back to the lodge when these four wanted to stay put."

"Where were they?"

"South Mine."

Ellory winced. The terrain around the mines was left rugged on purpose in the hope of discouraging exploration by guests. The mines weren't safe, and signs announced that, but they could serve as shelter in a pinch. A very dangerous pinch.

"Did you see a trail or any sign of him?" Mira would want to know everything, so she tried to anticipate questions.

"There is a trail, but it's the one that they followed in. If he's wise and we're lucky, he'll follow it back. There's still a chance that he'll make it back to the lodge while we're out looking for him. If he does, I need you to call on the radio and let me know. It was impossible to take the snowmobiles directly along that trail, but we're going to go back out and look. We'll take a quick peek in the mines between here and there, and hit South Mine again in case he went back to where they all were."

"After the storm?"

"No." He looked back and called to the group, all of whom had dove into the drinks and stew to fortify themselves. "Ten minutes and then we're going back out."

"You can't!" Ellory said, much louder than she'd intended. She tried again, quieter, calmer than she felt. "The storm is going to get really bad."

"We have some time." His voice had a gravelly sound that sent warm sparks over her ears, almost like a touch. That kind of voice would sound crazy sexy in whispers, hot breath on her ear... Raspy and...

"I'm sorry, what did you say? I think I misheard you." Or hadn't heard him at all. God, she had to do better than this.

"Are you a doctor?" he repeated.

"No." It was time for him to figure out she wasn't important, or capable of handling this.

"Where's Dr. Dupris?"

She noticed him looking back at the people in front of the fire, all out of their suits now, which meant time for step two.

Ellory spun and headed for the guests, expecting him to follow. "She's here, but I'm like triage or something. I have a list of things to wake her up for. And we have water heated in case there were any frostbite cases. Also I read that heating the feet would help get the body temperatures up fast. Actually, I have the saunas roaring too if that would help. I just wasn't sure whether or not that would be a bad thing or a good thing, and it wasn't in the books. Do you know?" She didn't stop, just threw the question out and then went on.

Since the staff had handled her warming requests, she headed for the smallest member of the party, a petite, pixie-like woman who wasn't drinking her cocoa…and who held her hands above her lap as if they were hurting.

His stride longer, he overtook her and scooped

up a stethoscope as he passed the tray of first-aid and examination supplies she'd laid out and slung the thing around his neck. Catching it caused a brief flash of pain on his handsome features. He ignored the pain, but Ellory noticed. That was her real job: Physio and massage therapy. Just not today.

He wasn't the concern right now. He'd been mostly warm when out there in it, though his cheeks looked chapped from the winter winds...

She reached down to gently lift one of the woman's arms to get a better look at her fingers. "What's your name, honey?"

"Chelsea," she answered, teeth chattering. "My fingers and toes burn. Like they're on fire."

"Socks off, everyone. Time to check extremities." Chelsea's fingertips were really red. Ellory didn't want to touch them, but she didn't really know enough about medicine not to investigate fully. Maybe frostbite started with redness?

Gingerly, she wrapped her hands over Chelsea's fingertips, causing the freezing woman to gasp in pain but confirming that they were indeed hot. This wasn't frostbite. Though that was probably going to be the next stage. "I'm sorry," she whispered, and let go of the hands, her gaze drifting down to where Angry Leader had knelt at Chelsea's feet, which he now examined. Her toes were exactly the opposite in color from her fingertips: an unnatural, disturbing, somewhat corpse-like white.

That might be a good reason to call Mira…

"Is that—?" She hadn't got the question out before he nodded and looked Chelsea in the eye.

"My name is Dr. Graves. Anson, if you prefer. I'll even tell you my middle name later if you need some more names to cuss me with… This isn't going to be pleasant. We have to warm your feet fast," Anson said, his raspy voice much gentler with the woman. "You have the beginning stages of frostbite."

Chelsea's gaze sharpened and she blurted out, "Are my toes going to fall off?" She sounded so stricken every head in the lobby turned toward her.

Ellory's heart skipped.

Anson looked grim and his wind-burned cheeks lost some of their color, but he shook his head. "It's going to feel like it. It will hurt like probably no one but you can imagine right now, but that's how you get to keep them." He didn't sugarcoat it, not even a hint of the usual *discomfort* nonsense doctors liked to say.

Chelsea nodded, her eyes welling.

Anson looked at Ellory again. "Get her pants off. How hot is the water?"

"One hundred and ten on the burners." Ellory answered. That she knew.

He looked surprised they'd been using a thermometer on it. "A little too hot. Add a small amount of cold water to it to get it to one hundred and five and then pour. It's got to be between one hundred and one hundred and five degrees Fahrenheit all the time. Dip out water, pour more in, or swap out the containers to keep it within range. I know that's going to be hard to do in buckets, but it needs to be done as exactingly as possible for a full half-hour." Anson said this to Ellory, who nodded and relayed the orders to her kitchen helpers, then helped Chelsea out of the bottom half of her suit.

By the time Chelsea was down to her thermals, the water had been sufficiently cooled and poured into a large rubber container. Ellory pushed the cotton cuffs to Chelsea's knees and guided the woman's feet into the water.

It hurt. She could tell by the way Chelsea's lower lip quivered, though admirably she didn't cry out.

With all the time Ellory had spent in disaster zones, witnessing human suffering, she should have built up some kind of callus to it by now, but it tore at her heart all the same. "I'm so sorry this has happened to you... We'll get you something for the pain."

"My fiancé is still out there," she whispered, clarifying in those simple words what hurt worse right now.

Ellory put one arm around Chelsea's shoulders, giving her a squeeze. "Let's get your insides warmed up and see if we can beat the shivering." She took the cocoa Chelsea hadn't been drinking and held it to her lips. "We'll help you with this until your fingers stop smarting and you can do it yourself, okay?"

"*Ohh*...chocolate," Chelsea said.

"That's pretty much how I feel about chocolate too." Ellory lifted the cup to the woman's mouth. "Sometimes it's the only thing that makes the stuff we have to go through bearable. Though I do feel like I should apologize for not making it from better ingredients." A nervous laugh bubbled up. "You didn't do anything wrong, that's not why I'm making you drink preservative juice." She was doing that thing again, where she lost control of her mouth because she was nervous.

Chelsea looked at her strangely. "Preservative juice?"

She named the popular brand of cocoa everyone knew, then added, "I'm sure it's fine. I'm just…" What could she say to explain that? "I'm big on organic."

"Ahh." Chelsea nodded, relaxing back in her chair.

Great bedside manner. Most of her patients worked with her for a long stretch of time so they got to know her quirks and oddities, and only had to suffer her help with exercise and a program that their physiotherapist designed. All Ellory did was help them through it and massage away pain, she didn't need to be trusted to make decisions.

Ellory added in what she hoped was a more agreeable tone, "Ignore me. It's a throwback to childhood."

"You were big on organic in childhood?" Anson

asked from down where he crouched, examining the feet of another patient. Which meant he was listening, and probably losing faith in her with every word that tumbled out of her mouth.

"Yes. In a manner of speaking."

His eyes were focused on the patient, but it still felt like he was staring at her. "Which is?"

The only way out of this conversation was to pretend it wasn't happening.

Stop. Talking.

Handing Chelsea's cup to another staff member, she said, "Please assist Chelsea with her cocoa. I should assist Dr. Graves." The man needed a different last name. Which she wouldn't bring up. She probably already sounded like an incompetent idiot to them.

She caught up with him kneeling before the last of the rescued, checking extremities.

As she stepped to his side he looked up, locking eyes with her in a way that said he knew she'd heard him and that he wasn't going to press the matter.

Message delivered, he got back to work and the potency of his stare dissipated. "Get all their feet into the water. But Chelsea's the only one you have to keep in the temperature range."

"What about the sauna?" She rolled with his return to business. As out of her depth as she felt, she did want to do a good job, take good care of them all.

"Maybe later, or if they don't get warm enough to stop shivering soon, but I'd rather you not put them into the stress of a sauna until a doctor is on hand should things get hairy."

Ellory nodded.

"I'm going to check on my crew. And Max."

Hearing his name, the fuzzy black dog currently stretched in front of the fire popped up and looked at Anson.

"Or maybe I'll get him some water first..." He called to the rescuers to check their feet and while they peeled off boots he took care of himself and the big bushy dog.

Ellory organized the helpers with instructions on the water, her shoulders growing tighter and tighter every time she looked through the door or the windows at the worsening storm. After assigning two people to Chelsea and getting them another round of hot blankets, she finally went to find Anson.

And Max—maybe the dog would listen to her concerns.

CHAPTER TWO

"WHAT IF YOU'RE not back in half an hour, when they come out of the warm water? And isn't that weird, a doctor moonlighting as a rescuer?" She'd always considered Mira to be an unusual doctor—fabulous and outdoorsy—so Anson seemed like an anomaly. He had the bossy bit down, at least. But he could be safe and inside during this weather, or out driving his four wheel drive and…smoking cigars. Whatever people did in four wheeled drives, she wasn't sure.

"Dry them gently and wrap them in loose gauze." He answered that first, then added, "I don't moonlight. I work in the ER six months of the year, and the rescue team is my life during ski season."

His admission surprised her. Adrenaline junkie? Extreme sports wackadoo? Both those fit the idea of returning to the outdoors in this weather. Once more, her gaze was pulled to the glass doors.

The snow, already heavy before they'd returned, had picked up even worse since. "Are you sure it wouldn't be better for you all to wait until the storm passes?"

The sharpness that came to his green eyes shut down that thought process completely. Right. He didn't say anything. He didn't need to.

Anson turned to his crew instead. "Five minutes." He pulled a plastic baggie from his pocket and extracted some kind of jerky to give to the big shaggy dog.

One of the group asked, "Where are we going?"

"Blue Mine and South Mine," Anson answered, then looked at Ellory. "Why are you not dressed for the weather?"

"I haven't bought clothes for being home yet, and all the winters in the past decade, I guess, have been in warm places. Before New Year's Eve I was in Peru. It's summer there right now. I wasn't sure if I was going to stay, so I didn't want to buy clothes I might not wear very long. It's wasteful."

He shook his head. "Rent a snow suit when you're going to be out in the elements…what's your name?"

"Ellory. And I have one." It's the one thing she did have, but it was old, hopelessly out of fashion and not nearly as well suited to the winter as the suits these people wore because she didn't wear manufactured materials. So it was bulky, and kind of itchy. And she left it at her parents' after every New Year…so it was musty from storage and…

She didn't need to share that with Anson. He was covered in layers of modern insulating materials, and while she could understand it and tried not to be jealous of his warmth and mobility, he wouldn't understand if she explained. Not that his opinion should matter. "I wasn't going out to stay in the weather earlier, just to meet you all. And I have thermal underwear under this."

Like he would think well of her if she'd been wearing wool and a parka in her short jaunt into the weather to meet them. She was a flake. That's how normal people viewed her. So today she was a flake who didn't dress properly. What else was new?

"Go put it on."

Ellory didn't know how to respond to a direct order like that. And she really didn't like it that the bossiness made her tingle again… Wrong time, wrong place, wrong feelings.

She wanted to blame them on her nerves too, like being nervous amplified all her other emotions, but she couldn't even lie to herself on that. Ruggedly handsome wasn't a look the man was going for—he just had it. Some combination of good genes, lifestyle and that voice gave it to him. She tried to ignore that, and the squirmy feeling in her belly she got when his mossy hazel eyes focused on her.

"Anson." She went with his name, in an attempt to reclaim some power. "It's not just blowing more, it's falling thicker. If you guys get all… frozen and stuff, then you aren't going to help find—"

"There's still time." He cut her off. Again.

Rude. Curt. Terse. That should make him less attractive. That should definitely make him feel like less of a threat to her stupid resolution…

He had flaws. The bossy thing, which shouldn't be hot. What else? He probably wasn't even half as strapping and impressive as his winter wear made him seem. It was just the illusion of beefy manliness from the cardinal rule of winter: loose layers kept you warmer. It somehow amplified the squareness of his jaw and the scruff that confirmed the dark color of the hair currently hidden by his knit cap.

Her heart rate accelerated and her hands waffled at her side. This was not going the way she'd pictured it while waiting and watching through the windows. She didn't anticipate having to try and convince someone not to go back out in the storm, and for some reason she knew he wouldn't care that she was more afraid for the crew than for the missing man.

She could just lock the door and keep everyone safe inside. Except she hated confrontation, and if he told her to give him the key in that bossy gravel voice of his, she'd give it to him. And possibly her undies too.

She could really think of a good way to distract him. It definitely violated her Stupid Resolution parameters, but it was in the name of humanity and keeping people safe. Surely that was a good reason for an exception.

Through all this stupidity, the only communication Ellory managed was skittish hand motions that made her jangle from the stacks of thin silver bangles she loved. Sentinels probably didn't jingle.

He glanced down at her hand and then back up, impatient brows lifting, urging her to say something else. Only Ellory didn't know what else to say.

Winter was his job after all. And, really, she'd spent most of the past lots of years in places where her weather awareness had mostly consisted of putting on sunscreen and seeking high ground during the rainy season. She probably wasn't the best judge of snow stuff.

When she failed to form any other words he started talking instead. Instructions. Things she'd already learned from studying Mira's medical books when reading up on treatment for frostbite and hypothermia. But it was good to hear it from someone who really knew something about it. Anything about it.

He even gave her additional explanations about signs of distress, outside the cold temperature illness symptoms she'd read about—other stuff to look for that would require Mira immediately, and he capped off the instructions with a long, measuring look. "If you're not up to the task, tell me now. I'll get Dr. Dupris down here."

"I'm up to the task." She was, she just wished she wasn't. "Are you? Your shoulder is hurt. I've seen you roll your arm in the socket at least three times since you came inside and you've been rubbing it too."

He closed the bag of dog treats and stuffed it into his pocket. "I'm all right. We'll call if we get stuck. And we've got survival gear on the ATVs."

Movement behind her made her aware that the team had all moved toward the door, ready to go wherever Fearless Leader told them to. They all either ignored what she'd been saying about the danger of going out in the crazy falling snow or were busy building an imaginary snow fort of denial.

Anson held the door and looked at the dog. "Max." One word and his furry companion scampered right out behind them.

It would be okay. People who risked their lives for others had to build up good karma. The team would make it back, and maybe their karma would extend to the still missing skier. Until then she'd do her best—manage the lobby/exposure clinic, keep the fire stoked and the water heated and flowing, and keep those who'd been out in it warm and safe.

After the team returned, and when the head count was official, then she'd get Mira.

Anson Graves's snowmobile crept through the falling white flakes. Theoretically, there should be another couple of hours of daylight left, but between the dense clouds and miles of sky darkened by falling snow it felt more like twilight. Zero visibility. He was half-afraid he'd find the missing man by accidentally running him over.

A trip that normally took fifteen minutes was taking forever.

Anson knew only too well how much longer it would seem for the man who was stuck in the cold, counting his own heartbeats and every painful breath, wondering how many more he'd have before the wind froze him from the inside and winter claimed him.

That's what he'd done.

The blonde at the lodge hadn't been wrong, he'd just wanted her to be wrong. At least half an hour had passed since they'd started the trek to the third-closest abandoned silver mine, and they weren't even halfway there yet. She should be getting Chelsea's feet out of the water and bandaging them by now. He'd forgotten to tell her not to let Chelsea walk...though maybe she wouldn't try.

If they hadn't had to take the long way they'd be there by now. But this was the safest route with the snow drifting the way it was.

If the wind would just stop...

The wet, blasting snow built a crust on his goggles, his eyes the only places not actively painful and cold from the wind. He shook his head, trying to clear the visor, but had to use his hand to scrape it off. He didn't even want to see what was becoming of Max in the back. Snow stuck to his fur like nothing Anson had ever seen.

The only thing he felt good about right now was leaving the four rescues with the hippie chick. Her choice of attire showed a distinct lack of common sense, but she'd picked up on his shoulder bothering him. She was perceptive and paying attention. And he'd seen her hug his frostbite patient. She cared. They'd be safe with her, especially considering the detailed instructions he'd given. She'd be watching them with an eagle eye for any slight changes. Getting Dupris should an emergency arise would be a simple enough task for anyone.

His stomach suddenly churned hard, a split second before he felt an unnatural shifting of the snow beneath him.

He reacted automatically, cutting sharply up the slope, and didn't stop until the ground felt firm beneath him. Damned sliding snowdrifts.

He'd only reacted in time because he'd been waiting for it to happen. After his harrowing experience, snow had become an obsession to him—learning the different kinds of snow, what made it slide, what made blizzards, all that. And since he'd bought Max and had him trained, he'd probably spent more time on the snow than anywhere else in his life. His instinct was honed to it, and he knew to listen to his gut.

Especially when he couldn't see the terrain well enough to judge with his eyes…

But he couldn't trust that his crew would have the same ability, especially with how tired they already were.

Conditions had just officially gotten too bad to continue.

His team had stopped when he'd pulled his maneuver—quickly enough to see how he'd survived it before they tried to follow—but he didn't want them to try it. They'd follow where he led, but he couldn't have any more lives on his conscience.

Grabbing the flashlight off his belt, he clicked it on, assuring that they'd see the motion even if they couldn't clearly see any other details, and gave it a swirl before pointing back in the direction from which they'd come.

Retreat.

He waited until they had all turned around and then started up the slope in a gentle arc to bring up the rear. Not ideal. The best formation had him at the front—taking the dangers first—but at least from this vantage he'd be able to see if anyone fell behind or started having difficulty.

He felt shifting against the cage at his back. Max huddled behind Anson, strategically placing himself to get the least of the cold wind that blasted around his owner, even as the machine crept along.

If it were just him, he'd stay out on the mountain, looking until it was impossible to do anything else, but there were five other human lives under his protection, not to mention his hard-working, life-saving dog.

"I'm sorry, man," he said to the wind.

They had to go back.

He'd have to tell the others they couldn't reach the mine. Yet.

They hadn't gotten far enough to find anyone or signs. Those they'd rescued earlier would just have to understand.

His gut twisted. He'd lost people to avalanches, recently even. But he'd never lost someone to a storm and not found them alive.

Worse, he'd have to lie to those people who'd been through so much. Say he was certain they would pick up the trail again as soon as the snow and wind let up. But the only thing he was certain of was the fear and guilt tearing through him—colder than the Colorado cyclone buffeting them about the mountainside.

Just as Anson had expected, Ellory was doing the job she'd been assigned. She'd been fast out the door when they'd first arrived, but not when they returned.

As quickly as they could, the team shut down

their machines, climbed off, and hurried inside. They hadn't been out in the weather that long compared to their hours of searching for the group, but the wind speeds were now enough that the awning over the front doors sounded like thunder as it rippled in the wind. That, coupled with exhaustion, made it impossible to keep warm.

He stepped through the ornate doors to the comforting heat and the smell of burning wood. The fireplace in the lobby still burned actual wood, something that had surprised him when he'd returned to Silver Pass. It was good. Wood fire dried out the air and cut through the damp better than anything but a shower. Anson loved the crackling and the temperatures for those times, like now, when he just couldn't get warm enough. The dancing flames. The red coals. The warm golden light, so hopeful… Hopefulness he wished he felt.

Max looked up at him, made eye contact, and then headed for the fireplace at a trot. He always did that and Anson still didn't know whether it was him asking for permission to do something, or he was just giving Anson a heads-up that he was going.

His crew hit the hot beverages first, the fastest way to heat up your core, leaving Anson to check on his patients and deliver the news.

Ellory had positioned his frostbite patient close to the fire, having transferred her to a fancy brass wheelchair that matched the décor—the lodge kept a few on hand for the really bad skiers— and now sat at Chelsea's feet, gently patting them dry. She'd kept them in the hot water bath longer than he'd told her to. Not great. The tissue was fragile and being waterlogged wouldn't do her any favors.

A hot plate sat on the floor about a foot away, which was new. Somewhere closer to keep the water hot for the footbath.

She was taking that temperature range very seriously at least. Probably keeping it better than the whirlpool baths at the hospital.

"Chelsea's toes are pink now," Ellory called, on seeing him. It almost helped. "Well, almost all the way pink. A couple of her small toes have a bit of yellow going on. We had a little trouble with the water temperature at first, but once we moved the hot plate closer, it got easier to keep it in the range."

"It's not hurting as bad now," Chelsea added in quiet tones, swiveling in her chair to look the lobby over.

She was looking for her fiancé, as they all were, but she was the one who'd be hurt the most if the man didn't make it back.

Anson stepped around and crouched to look at her toes. "No blisters have formed yet, so that's good. You'll likely get a couple of blisters soon, when they start swelling. But we're going to take good care of you, and when the storm passes we'll get you to a hospital."

"What about Jude?" Chelsea asked, letting him know what she was interested in talking about but not whether she'd heard him at all. Someone would have to repeat the information to her later.

Anson straightened so he could address the group. "The storm has gotten to the point where it's impossible for us to continue searching. I want to be clear: this is just a suspension of the search, not the end of it. I'm sorry we haven't found your fiancé yet."

"Jude." Chelsea repeated the name of the missing skier, stopping Anson with one hand on his arm.

"Jude," he repeated, his pulse kicking up a little higher. He knew why it was important to her, but saying the man's name made it harder to maintain the distance he needed to be smart about this. "Just because we have to postpone going back out to look for Jude, it doesn't mean it's time to give up hope. So don't get ahead of us, okay? You'd be surprised what someone can survive. Those mines are a pretty good shelter. There are also some rocky overhangs between here and where we found you. And some of those might actually be better."

"How could they be better? You're closer to the snow," one of the rescued asked.

He contemplated how much to actually tell them about his experience with this kind of situation. *I know these things, I killed someone with snow once* wouldn't inspire anyone to trust him. This had to be about them, not about his fear or guilt. "Small spaces hold the warmth your body makes better, and the wind can't get into it as fully as it does in the mines, which have a bigger entrance and room for the wind to move around inside. He might still show up here before we get out to him, but as soon as the storm lets up we'll get back out there. It's not time to give up hope." He repeated that, trying to convince himself.

It was time to bandage Chelsea's toes…and hopefully him moving on would make them take the hint not to ask more questions. He didn't have any answers or much of a mind left for coming up with more empty words of comfort. He was too busy trying to ignore the similarities between this storm and *his* storm.

Pulling off his cap and gloves, he squatted beside Ellory at Chelsea's feet, struggling to hold his calm for everyone else. "Do you have some gloves for me to use?"

Ellory ducked into the bag of supplies she'd packed and fished out the box of gloves. One look at them confirmed they wouldn't do. Small. He could squeeze into a medium at a pinch, but large were better. "All right, this job has been passed to you."

To his surprise, she didn't argue at all, just grabbed a couple gloves from the box and put them on. Crouched so close he was enveloped in a cloud of something fruity and floral. The woman looked like summer, and she smelled like spring.

Warm. And distracting. He scooted to the side to give her room.

"What is the job?" she asked, looking at Chelsea's toes and maneuvering herself so she could gently cradle the patient's heel in her lap.

He handed the gauze to her and began ripping strips of tape and tacking them to the wheelchair, where she could get to them. "Part of the healing process is just keeping the site dry and loosely bandaged." He gave short, quick instructions, and left her to it.

She unrolled the gauze carefully and began wrapping. He watched, ready to correct her, but she did it as he would've: a couple of passes between the two toes to keep them separate, controlling the moisture level better, and then loosely around the two together.

No matter how out of her depth she looked, she was anything but incompetent. There might even be some kind of medical training there. The cloud of floral scent stole up his dry, burning sinuses and almost made his mouth water like a dog's.

Awesome priorities. Reveling in attraction to some woman while the lost man was freezing. Maybe dying. He definitely didn't have the warm comfort of a fireplace and a wench-shaped blonde to take his mind off his failure to get back to the lodge safely, didn't even know his friends had been saved, so he suffered that additional torment—worry for them in addition to himself.

An inferno of shame ignited in his belly.

Hide it.

At the very least he owed them all a confident appearance. Calm. Strength. Determination.

Meltdowns were something to have alone—a luxury that would have to wait until he was no longer needed.

CHAPTER THREE

ELLORY HAD READ about frostbite treatment so she could anticipate Dr. Graves's needs for that, but she had no idea what his other needs were. She'd kind of pegged the search and rescue team as attracting the kind of adrenaline fiends in it for the thrill, but Anson looked almost as devastated by returning empty-handed as Chelsea had.

With the bandage applied, she switched off the hot plate, scooted it out of the way and stood. What came next? She didn't know, but certainly there would be something she would need to do, and being on her feet would help her react that much faster.

"They still hurt, I know," Anson said to the woman, looking at the toes now hidden by the gauze, the patch of yellow skin surrounded by angry redness hidden. "But most of this might not even be frostbite. The yellow area is, but the good news is that we got to it in good time and it's very unlikely to leave any lasting damage. I won't be able to tell for a couple of days if it's frostbite or the lesser version, which you all have on your fingers and toes...frostnip. We're going to treat yours as if you have frostbite, just to be safe. I'll see what kind of antibiotics Dr. Dupris has in her inventory, and some pain medication."

Good news. She'd take whatever kind of win they could get.

Anson asked the standard allergy questions, got whatever info he needed, and nodded once to Ellory—a kind of *do it* nod. She had been promoted: triage to assistant, or nurse...or whatever that position was.

"I can check with Mira. Which antibiotic do you need?" If she had to, she could no doubt find in Mira's books which kind of antibiotic was good for skin infections, but she'd rather he tell her. She wasn't a doctor. Not by a long stretch. But she knew enough to know that antibiotics were a tricky lot—some worked for everything, some worked best for specific things, and these days a frightening amount were resistant to stuff they used to be awesome at fighting.

"I'm sure she's got some of the broad-spectrum

ones, but I don't know how well the drug cabinet is stocked for anything obscure." For some reason she wanted him to think well of her, and she felt more competent even saying the words "broad spectrum." Like proving to him she wasn't a complete idiot was important. Probably something to do with the lecture she'd gotten about her clothes...

She didn't even know the man, had never seen him before today, but as he spoke she became aware of something else: there was a rawness about him she couldn't name. Something in that raspy timbre that resonated feelings primal and violent.

He rattled off a few medication names that sounded like gibberish to her, and she didn't ask him to repeat himself, just hoped she could remember them when she came face-to-face with a wall of gibberish-sounding drug names.

Then she'd come back here and keep an eye on the good doctor with the terrible name, because alarm bells were ringing in her head.

Chelsea suffered the whole situation with more dignity than Ellory could've mustered, and directed the conversation back to what she really wanted to talk about. "If I got frostbite in the mine and I wasn't in the snow, Jude's going to have it for sure, isn't he?"

"Nothing is ever certain." Ellory said it too quickly. It sounded like a platitude. She shook her head and tried again with better words. "You can't compare your situation to his for a couple of reasons: women don't hold heat as well as men do, and your boots are different. Even if they are the same brand, the fit will be different. If his have more room inside than yours they'll hold heat better. If he's taken shelter in a smaller space than you did, like Anson...Dr. Anson...was saying, he could just be warmer..."

Anson pulled out the footrests on the wheelchair and carefully positioned Chelsea's feet on the metal tray. "Find a pillow for her."

Ellory knew he was speaking to her, even though he didn't look at her. She hurried to the main desk and the office behind, where she knew she'd find some. When she presented him with two slender pillows from the office, he put one under Chelsea's feet and rose. "Would you like the other pillow to sit on?"

"Yes." She made as if to rise and Anson put his

hands out to stop her. "No walking. No standing. When you need to go to the bathroom, someone's going to have to go with you. Right now, I've got you. Luckily, you weigh about as much as a can of beans…" He caught her under the arms and lifted. Ellory slid the pillow beneath and then stood back as he returned Chelsea to her seat, lifting a brow pointedly at him when she saw his shoulder catch again and a wave she could actually name cross his handsome features: pain. His shoulder definitely hurt.

She really had to stop thinking about how hot he was. It wasn't helping at all. It wasn't breaking her resolution to think that the untouchable doctor rescue guy was hot, but it might lead her to other thoughts. It also wasn't her fault that his eyes looked like moss growing on the north side of a tree…deep, earthy green blending to brown. Was that hazel or still green if she looked…?

He was staring at her. It took a couple of nervous heartbeats for her to realize that it wasn't because he was a mind-reader.

Oh, yeah, she'd made the *Ahh, your shoulder does hurt* face at him. Because it did. He'd made the pain face, she'd made the *ahh* face, and now he was making the scowl face.

He didn't know she was sexually harassing him in her mind.

While she was trying to decide what she was supposed to be thinking, the man pivoted and walked straight through the archway leading to the rest of the resort.

Where was he going?

Crap.

She should have gone after the medicine by now.

He was going to disturb Mira, maybe make her leave the love nest and come down here.

"I'll be back in a few minutes, Chelsea," she babbled, and rushed after him in a flurry of flowing skirts and jingling bracelets, but she was too late to see which direction he'd headed. The elevators all sat on the bottom floor, where she was.

The man was a ninja. A cranky, frosty ninja.

Ducking into the stairwell, Ellory tilted her head to listen, hoping he wasn't outside earshot. The plush carpeting that blanketed the hallways and stairs made it hard to tell which way he'd gone.

"Anson?" Tentative call unanswered, she stepped back into the hallway.

Okay, so he didn't go upstairs by any means, he wasn't heading for Mira and Jack's suite.

Mira's office? He did want antibiotics for Chelsea. She turned to the right, the shorter hallway, gathered her skirts to her knees so they'd stop the damned swirling, and ran. No yelling. Yelling disturbed people. And every single person in the lodge, except for maybe the two upstairs sheltered from all this information overload in their love nest, were disturbed enough with the current situation.

One turn and then another, she reached the final hallway just in time to see Anson reach the end and turn toward the wall outside the clinic.

Before she could call out to him, he reared back and slammed his fist through the drywall.

The loud slam and cracking sound stunned her into staring for a couple of seconds. Long enough for the pain to reach his brain and make him pull his hand out of the hole while the other gripped his poor shoulder. If it hadn't hurt before he'd done that...

"You broke the wall," she muttered as she trotted forward, no longer running. She was not at all sure how to respond to this masculine and aggressive display. She didn't know anyone who hit walls when they were upset. Generally, she kept company with people who avoided violence. "I have the keys to Mira's office, we can get whatever you need for Chelsea. I've been keeping an inventory of supplies."

He finally turned to look at her and she saw it again—he wasn't just upset. She saw desolate, blind torture in his hollow eyes. It robbed her of any ability to speak.

Whatever she'd thought earlier about his motivation behind taking this kind of work, she was now certain: It had nothing to do with being an adrenaline junkie or any kind of fixation on the dream of being the big hero. This mattered to him. This *hurt* him.

She did the only thing she could, reached out and touched him. Tried to ground him here with her.

Contact of her palm with his stubble-roughened cheek sharpened his gaze, bringing him back from wherever he'd gone.

"Don't worry about the wall. We'll fix it. Everything will be okay." She whispered words meant to soothe him.

It took him a few seconds, but his brows relaxed and he nodded, looking down at the bloody knuckles on his hand and then at the wall. "That was pretty stupid. She's going to give me hell, isn't she?" He mustered a smile while simultaneously pulling his head back from her hand.

He didn't want her touching him… Okay. It's not like they really knew one another, and some people just didn't like to be touched.

It wasn't about her. It wasn't judgment on her.

Ellory pulled her thoughts away from the vulnerable nerve he'd accidentally struck and played along, faking a grin with her tease. "You have no idea. She's going to make you cry like a baby."

His smile was equally slight, but it was a start. And it reminded her of where she should make him focus. Sobering, she reached for his hand but didn't touch him, a request, open palms. "Can I see it?"

Okay, that might've been a test.

She'd been rejected more times in her life than any person ought to be—it wasn't anything new to her—but the second she'd found out that he was a doctor he'd become her partner in dealing with this and keeping Mira out of it. She needed him to actually connect with her and be her partner in it. And a good person didn't abandon her partner when he was hurting.

When he placed his large, bloody-knuckled hand in hers, her relief was so keen she had to fight the urge to squeeze and wind her fingers in his. He didn't shun her. Recoiling was about something else. He didn't find her lacking.

Nice skin, and considering she hadn't had any male contact since she'd come back from Peru it wasn't surprising that she wanted to relish the contact a little bit.

She forced herself to examine his knuckles before he caught on, paying careful attention to the cracked and rapidly swelling skin. "Can you move your fingers for me?"

He made a small sound as he got his fingers going, but his fingers moved smoothly at the knuckle, despite the swelling. "Well, we both know that it's an old wives' tale that you can't move something that's broken. Can't know for sure that it's not, but it looks good. Sorry, have to do this…"

Still holding his injured hand for support, she stroked her fingers over the abused skin, just firmly enough to feel the structure. She knew it hurt, he stopped breathing until she stopped touching it. "Don't think it's broken. Everything feels intact. Could be some hairline fracture, though. Guess we'll have to take a wait-and-see approach on this, along with poor Chelsea's toes."

Breathing resumed, and he pulled his hand back, nodding. "I don't think it's broken either, but I'm a fan of X-ray..."

"Come on. Let's get this cleaned up, then we'll get Chelsea's medicine into her, and I'll go and tell Mira what's going on so she can join the fun later. While the storm is here, you two will keep watch over our patient guests in shifts so she can have time with Jack and you can have some rest. Welcome to your first rotation at Silver Pass Blizzard Clinic, Dr. Graves."

"Time with Jack?" he asked, as she turned toward the door.

Ellory fished the keys from her coat pocket, unlocked the door and stepped inside, flipping on one set of lights as she went. "The past six months have been really hard for Mira, not that she'd admit it to anyone. Her fiancé was a louse. They broke up and the universe rewarded her for choosing to take care of herself."

"Jack from the avalanche, or do you mean her reward is having to do jack-all?"

Ellory peered at him. "Have you never heard the name Jack before?"

"I have and I've met a guest called Jack. But it's also a noun or an adjective." He followed her into the clinic. "Your manner of speaking is un-usual. I'm looking for landmarks."

She decided not to comment on that—he didn't seem like a big talker and she had jobs before her. She talked strangely. She dressed wrong. Blah-blah-blah.

"I've been making notes of the supplies I took to the lobby. We'll just write down whatever we need, I'll go tell Mira and you can get the medi-cine for Chelsea. We should probably start charts for everyone too, but since your hand looks like hell, you tell me what you want it to say and I'll do the writing."

Anson followed her, enjoying the floral wake. The tropical scent reminded him she'd said something about Peru earlier. "Were you on a medical mission before you came here?"

She unlocked the drug cabinet and opened the doors, then flipped on a light above it and pointed at the bottles to direct his attention. "Medical mission? Oh, no. You mean in Peru. No, I was at a..." She looked sidelong at him, her expression growing wary. "I was at an ayahuasca retreat."

The word was familiar somehow, but between the pain in his hand, the pain in his shoulder and the headache he'd been nursing since he'd decided to turn the group around he couldn't place it. "I know I should know what that is, but it's eluding me."

"It's a place you go to have..." She stumbled along, clearly hedging and not really wanting to tell him.

People who avoided a direct answer had something to hide, either because it embarrassed them or they expected disapproval. Which was when he remembered what ayahuasca was. "Ayahuasca is a hallucinogen, isn't it?"

Her sigh confirmed it. "It's not like LSD or hard drugs. It's a herbal and natural way of expanding your consciousness. I went there for a

spirit quest under the care of a shaman—someone who knows about use of the plant and how
to make the decoction properly. Someone who
could help me understand everything I needed
to know beforehand. And before you say anything, I'm not a drug user. I don't smoke anything.
I only drink alcohol once a year—champagne
on New Year's with Mirry. And nothing else remotely dodgy the rest of the year." As she spoke,
her volume increased, along with the tension between her brows. "My body is a freaking temple,
Judgy McGravedigger."

Anson lifted both hands, trying to put the brakes
on the situation before she got really angry. Obviously he'd hit a nerve, she'd gone from quiet and
somewhat babbly to angry because he'd called it
a hallucinogen. "I'm not judging, but I am curi-
ous. And I agree your body is a temple."

Smooth.

When she turned back to her task he focused
on the cabinet again and the array of medicines,
and changed the subject. "Well stocked."

She went with it and didn't comment on his
completely unacceptable remark about her body.
"Mirry's a planner. She likes to be prepared for

anything. She's always been good like that, never lets anyone down." A clipboard hung inside the cabinet, but where he'd expected to see an inventory sheet had been clipped a single piece of notebook paper, a list of supplies in a scrolling, extravagant script. She picked it up and began writing again.

Mirry? Always been?

Ellory wasn't a nurse…

Sister? "Are you Ellory Dupris?" Anson put the two names together as he plucked one bottle of antibiotics from the shelf and set it on her clipboard so she could get a good look at the spelling and dose of medication.

"Ellory Du…? Oh, no. My name is Ellory Star."

She scribbled down the medicine then put the bottle into a little plastic basket. "You look for any other medicines, I'm going to get the supplies to clean your knuckles up." Before she headed away she turned back to him with a little pinch between her brows. "I'm sorry I made fun of your name. It wasn't nice. But in my defense it's kind of a terrible name. You should change it. Pick something more positive."

Pick something? "You picked Star, didn't you?"

"Yep."

Okay… He'd think about that later. "You do work here, though."

"Licensed massage therapist, which is my primary occupation, I guess. I've completed training and passed boards to be a physiotherapy assistant in Texas, but I haven't done any office work on it or taken boards here. The closest I came was a mission where the leader had back trouble and I helped her with the daily exercises her actual treatment prescribed…helped her handle being out in the field," she answered, fishing a badge from under her sweater and answering the question that he'd been working toward.

Anticipating. She really was perceptive. And the occupations fit. But then again, she could've said artist, pagan priestess, or tambourine player and he would've believed her. So, a massage therapist who called the owner's daughter and resort doctor 'Mirry.'

He plucked another medication from the cabinet, the mildest prescription-level pain medicine Mirry…Dr. Dupris…had in stock, and put it on the clipboard. "I put another medicine there for pain for Chelsea. Frostbite pain is monstrous."

Shrugging out of his coat, he pushed his sleeves up and stepped over to the sink to wash his hands, paying special attention to the puffy and bloody knuckles. He gave his fingers a few more slow flexes. Burning. Tenderness. But no bone pain. He knew about bone pain, just as he knew about frostbite pain. So she was right, even without having that information at her disposal. Good eye.

"Oh, my God, that's all you…"

He turned away from the sink, hand still under the water. "What's all me?"

"I was hoping that the coat was puffier than it seems to be."

He briefly considered not asking her for clarification, but he needed all the information he could get to keep up in conversation with this woman. "Why were you hoping my coat was puffy?"

"You're seriously beefy. Shoulders a mile wide, muscled. It's going to make working on you hard. I was hoping that some of that was your gear, your coat… I've got pretty strong hands and upper body, but you're going to be a tough case." She'd put a tray on the table, an array of antiseptics, gauze, tapes and ointments on it, and then went to write the medicine on her special clipboard.

"No, I won't. I don't need to be worked on." He didn't mention the compliment. Best ignore that attraction she'd all but said was mutual.

"How's it feeling?"

Good. She wasn't going to push the subject. "Nothing broken but the wall and my self-control. Bruised. Some abrasions…" He dried his hands on paper towels and wandered toward the table. "Maybe a mild sprain." He'd hit the wall hard.

"After you give the medicine to Chelsea, I want you on my table."

"Ellory, I don't need it."

"Suffering for no reason doesn't make you tough, it makes you stupid." She made a noise he could only consider a verbal shrug, "Your shoulder needs working on. If you want that thing to heal up so you can get back out there to find Jude when the snow lets up, let me help you."

He should've seen that coming. Her vocation was one hundred percent hands on, and from what he could tell by having observed her, she was on a mission to take care of the world.

The idea had some appealing qualities. Not the least of which the prospect of having her hands on his body… She might be dressed like a crazy person, considering the season and latitude, and conversing with her might be like running a linguistic obstacle course, but strangely neither of those things made her unappealing. And neither did the revelation about her spirit quest.

But he didn't really deserve comfort, and it was possible that his shoulder would calm down on its own in a little while.

"Maybe later. I should stick around the lobby. Keep a watch on them and the weather."

"Have you seen the radar? The storm is going to be with us for a while, hours and hours. We'll leave one of the radios with your people in the lobby and they can call us if…" The lights flickered, stopping her flow of words and her hands. When the power steadied and stayed on, she continued, "We're going to lose electricity."

"Maybe. We should see about making preparations, on the off chance…"

"It's not an off chance, Anson. It happens in every bad storm that hits the pass. Summer. Winter. Doesn't matter what kind of storm. It's not the whole town, but the lines to the lodge are dodgy, always breaking or going out for some reason. Tree limbs. High winds. Accumulation of heavy snow or ice…"

"I thought you were just in Peru."

"And before that Haiti. And before that the Central African Republic. Before that Costa Rica. But I was born and raised in Silver Pass. I needed to come home after my retreat, and Mira offered me a place to work. I have a history with the lodge. I know what I'm talking about. Nothing ever changes here. The power *will* go out."

"What does a massage therapist do in those places?"

"Dig ditches. Build dams. Distribute food, clothing, or whatever the mission is. And I help at the end of the day when people are worn out and hurting from all the manual labor." She disappeared into the office, and after some mucking around in there came out with a file folder, some forms, and another clipboard. "And there have been a few projects where I ended up with the same project leader, and I think she took me along as much to help keep her on her feet as to help with the actual project."

She left him to clean and dress his hand and made some notes in Chelsea's chart.

She'd grown up at the lodge, which explained why she was on such intimate terms with the owners. "You knew Dr. Dupris growing up?"

"Yes, and before you dig further she's my best friend. I love her more than anyone else in the whole world and if I'm upsetting you by making you help with the skiers, or making you let me help you, you're just going to have to get over it. She's having some much-needed downtime, and I'm going to take care of her people. Right now you're one of them, Dr. Graves. So suck it up, get the medicine into Chelsea and meet me at the massage therapy room. It's three doors down. There's a sign." She locked the drug cabinet and then turned and tossed her keys to him.

He instinctively caught them with his right hand, and regretted it. The combination of flying metal hitting his throbbing palm and the quick jerk of his arm tweaking his shoulder doubled the pain whammy that followed.

"Fine." Not fine. Annoyed. But as annoying as it was, she had a point, and if she could help, he'd make use of her.

"Lock the door when you leave. And turn off the lights. No wasting fossil fuels."

At least she didn't gloat.

CHAPTER FOUR

WHEN ELLORY KNOCKED on Mira's door, she wondered if she would be interrupting something she didn't want to interrupt.

Not usually one to be shy about sex, Ellory could only blame her squeamishness on the fact that being around Anson was making her think naughty thoughts, and now she was acutely aware that she wasn't allowed to follow through with them.

She hadn't specifically said her resolution not to date included no hook-ups, but she was trying to break that cycle as she'd spent her adult life sublimating her desire for love with lots of sex. Safe, sterile sex. So in the spirit of the resolution it had to include hooking up with handsome, inexplicably surly, dog-owning doctors—because Anson and his mile-wide shoulders were the best Fling Contender in Silver Pass.

She scrambled out of the stairwell on the top

floor, already avoiding the elevators so she didn't get trapped when the power went off, and jogged down the corridor to Mira's Stately Pleasure Dome.

In the plus column, Anson would never want to date her, so her Stupid Resolution wasn't in danger. He'd already remarked on finding her strange—unsurprising as most people who didn't move in her circles found her odd. Add to that him now thinking she was someone who would use the spirit quest as a reason to go to the rainforest and take drugs…

But none of that came close to touching the biggest block: the anguish she'd seen in his eyes earlier didn't leave room for much thought of carousing.

Even if sex was a really good way to generate heat when the power cut out during a raging blizzard.

Also? Sheer entertainment value. Something else she'd ignore from here on.

None of that helped her figure out how to talk to Mira without being afraid that she was interrupting something special. More special than any sex Ellory had ever had…another reason she was weirded out about it.

Mira had found love. Real love… It wouldn't just be sex Ellory interrupted, it'd be making love—which was probably sacred.

Or, as she'd like to think of it, making wild, reality-shattering love so potent it could mess with physics, the future, the past, and maybe illuminate all those dark places in her heart where negative thoughts and bad feelings liked to hide.

She'd been looking hard for that for the past decade, but it was elusive.

She stopped in front of the carved white door of Number Five's fancy suite and did the unthinkable: She knocked. "I'm sorry, Mirry, I have to talk to you."

The sound of stumbling and doors closing preceded the door opening, and her decidedly disheveled best friend appeared in the frame. "Hey. Is everything okay?"

Bedhead. That glazed look that came with passion that's been unexpectedly shut down. She'd definitely interrupted love…

"I'm so sorry. I just want to keep you informed about what is going on, and there's some stuff.

But I want you to know that I'm handling it, and Anson too. I'm not handling Anson…well, I am a little. But not in a sexy way. I'm still being faithful to my resolution." Ellory stopped talking. That's not what she was supposed to talk about. "The blizzard."

Mira, gaze sharpening with understanding, unsuccessfully tried to hide a smile smug enough that Ellory knew she'd be getting teased to hell and back if Mira weren't likely in a hurry to get back to Jack. "Good to know you're handling Anson. What about the blizzard?"

"We've got missing people. Person. One. The others, the rescue team got back. They were suffering moderate hypothermia but we've got them warmed up and are keeping a close eye on all four of them. One of them has either stage one or stage two frostbite on her toes, Anson said. Did you know he's a doctor too? He's been treating her. We went and got medicine from the clinic, and I've written down—"

"I'll get dressed…"

"No!" Ellory grabbed her arm to keep her from getting away. "It's okay, really. We're doing great…except for the missing man, and you can't help with that right now. One of the guests who was with the rescued group tried to get back to the lodge on his own, and he didn't make it back before the storm, or yet, and they weren't able to locate him before the storm got too dangerous and the visibility too bad. It's impossible to go out right now. I knew you'd want to know, but there's nothing you can do about it right now. Later or tomorrow, if you want to come check on everyone, that'd be great. Anson is tired. I'd feel bad making him do like a seventy-two-hour shift or something."

"Where are they?"

"Still in the lobby in front of the blazing fire, but we're relocating them to the fireplace suites. The lights flickered so I figure we're going to lose the power and then the central heat will go…so I'm corralling everyone into the fireplace suites, employees too. Doubling up occupancy and stuff. Everything is as under control as it can be, there's nothing else you could do. Well, unless you know how to fix drywall."

"What happened to the drywall?" Mira, unlike everyone else in her world, didn't have any trouble keeping up with Ellory's mind—which could be counted on to bear off in another direction without warning during pretty much every conversation. But especially those fraught with emotion and where something unpredictable loomed.

"Anson punched it. There's a hole…"

"This isn't sounding all that under control, Elle."

"I know it sounds all kinds of chaotic, but that's because I'm condensing hours and hours into a few minutes. He's sorry about the drywall, but he's very upset and worried about Jude."

Mira nodded slowly, taking it all in. She didn't even have to ask who Jude was, she just kept up. "The lost skier…"

"I brought you this." Ellory fished a spare radio from her pocket and handed it over. "I know you'll want to be contacted super-fast if there is an emergency. They're all tuned to the lodge emergency channel, and they'll be spread out among the patient rooms and rescuers, so anyone in need of help can get it fast when the power goes out."

Ellory's faith in Mira was boundless, and generally that faith extended to the confidence Mira would mirror her own faith. Not many people did that. No one, actually. Not right now, at least. But for a few seconds while Mira considered the radio in her hands, Ellory's faith wavered. "I can do it, Mira. I won't let you down. I promise."

"I know. I know you can. I was just thinking about whether I'm taking advantage..."

Relief warmed her and she relaxed, a smile returning. "You're not taking advantage of anyone, except maybe Jack." Ellory shook her head, covering her friend's hand as she teased. "And don't worry about the hole in the wall. I'll get Anson all patched up and then I'll make sure that he fixes the wall or gets billed for putting his fist through it when everything is up and running. And speaking of running, I need to. I have him on my table."

"Anson?"

"He hurt his shoulder."

"With the wall..."

"Well, it was hurt before that. But he made it worse with the wall." Ellory smiled and gathered up her skirts. "Don't worry, I'm just going to work on his shoulder. Not breaking my Stupid Resolution! You're still losing this year, Dupris!" And since the wing was deserted and she wanted Jack to hear, Ellory bellowed, "But that's okay, your Karmic Love-Jackpot Sex Machine Jack sounds like a good consolation prize!" She backed down the hallway, smiling as Mira's cheeks went pink.

Karmic Love-Jackpot Sex Machine was a much better nickname than Number Five, even if it took forever to say. Any man should be proud to bear that title.

Anson unlocked the door to the massage room and stepped inside, flipping on the lights. It was warm in there. Warmer than anywhere else he'd been in the lodge, except rooms that had *steam* in the name.

He pulled the top of his snow suit off again and let it pool at his waist, then took a seat while waiting. Like everywhere else, it was a deeply comfortable room, with plush chairs, stacks of fresh towels, a line of oil bottles and lotions…and the lingering scent of sandalwood and eucalyptus. A hedonist paradise.

Luxury. Comfort. And he was getting a massage when he should be out looking for the lost skier… No, nothing at all wrong with that.

Ellory had a point about him being in top shape for when the snow let up, but he was wound so tight it'd be a miracle if she could get him to relax at all.

He even felt guilty about wanting to relax a little. His rational mind knew how big this storm was, that if they were lucky it would be over in a day, and that he couldn't spend all the time until then on watch for a break. There'd be no break until it was over. Resting and taking care of the patients until then was the correct course of action.

He'd be doing something, but he wanted to do something more active.

And doing anything kept him from having too much time to think about what the man was going through while *he* was warm, safe, and...resting.

He stood and headed for a shelf with candles. Light the candles, save time.

He also lit a stick of incense propped in a holder, because that probably had some kind of peace-making mojo she would insist he needed.

When he stumbled over a remote control, he turned on music from a well-hidden stereo system.

By the time he'd gotten everything powered up, the door opened and Ellory walked in, pulling back her long, wavy, sun-kissed locks as she did, and twisting them into some kind of knot at the nape of her neck.

"So you do want a massage." She smiled. "Got the candles going for mood lighting, the incense, the music…"

"I was helping. Speeding things up." And now he was making excuses. He shut up.

"Yes, you were helping, but I'm pretty sure there's only one lightning-fast method of instantly relaxing." She closed the door, locked it, set her radio on the counter and began stripping. Off came the coat. Then her sweater…which left her wearing a small white T-shirt that had risen up enough to give him a view of the curve of smooth hip to waist before her arms came back down and she was once more covered. "And while that was completely inappropriate, it was payback for earlier. Don't worry, we're not doing that."

Despite seeing him at less than his best, and witnessing him put his fist through the wall—which he really wasn't proud of—the little eco-princess was flirting with him. He smiled, felt it, thought better of it and stopped. No wonder the woman liked to go to tropical places. Golden, shapely, and not at all what the media would classify a beach body…in the best way.

"Why are you getting undressed, then?"

It might have been years since he had a massage from anyone other than a lover, but he was sure that the only person who got naked was the one getting ministered to.

"I don't want to get oil on my clothes." She tossed the sweater onto the couch. "I'll keep my skirt on and the thermals beneath, but the sweater's sleeves are baggy and tend to drag. Oil would ruin it." A brief pause and she gestured to the opposite corner of the room. "There's a changing room through there, just strip down and wrap a towel around your waist. Underpants on or off, up to you. And I'll get…"

What she was saying registered and he shook his head, moving to sit in a chair, "I don't need to change. It's just my shoulder."

"Okay. Take off your shirt, then. And your shoes. You're the only one who didn't have your toes checked when you came in."

"I don't need my toes checked," he muttered, that directive enough to pull him out of the fantastic place his mind was going. Perfect little beach body didn't need to gawk at his ugly feet. But now that he'd seen what was beneath the baggy sweater, he wanted to see what was beneath the flowing skirts.

"Shirt," Ellory repeated, done arguing with him for now. She'd work on his shoulder, get him to relax, and then get him on the table. She couldn't fix his shoulder without having full access to his back. It was all connected. Not that she was going to bring that up with him right now. He was a doctor, he knew full well how anatomy and muscles worked together. He was just being a pain in the butt, and there was no reasoning with a pain in the butt. Logic didn't win in an emotional kerfuffle and after seeing his display of testosterone earlier she could definitely say he was having an emotional kerfuffle he didn't want to talk about.

Out of the corner of her eye she could see him complying. Arms up, material moving... She didn't look yet. He may have lit incense, and there might be enough essential oils in this room to gag an apothecary, but with his suit open and body heat escaping, all Ellory could smell was Eau d'Yummy Masculinity.

All she needed was to start undressing him with her eyes. That would lead to her undressing him with her hands, and then her Stupid Resolution would be shot.

Distract him. She should talk about something.

"So, you ever been south of the equator?" And that sounded like another come on. Because he'd turned her hormones on.

"No, and I've never done drugs with a shaman either."

"It's not like that."

Eucalyptus. That was a manly smell, and it would overpower the warm, salty awesomeness pouring off him. She snatched up the bottle of oil, a couple of towels and headed his way. "Do you want to lie on the table?"

"No."

She rolled her eyes, and didn't even try to hide it from him. He countered with a brow lift. "You can reach my shoulder from here." He did slide forward in the chair so he was sitting at the front edge at least.

In an effort to save his snow suit from the oil, she shook out two towels, draping one over his lap and tucking the other into the wad of insulated material at his waist, then stepped between his legs and reached for the oil.

"The skin on your shoulder isn't bruised, unless it's such a deep bruise that it hasn't come out yet. Is that the case?"

"Doubt it."

"Okay, how did you injure it?"

"Lifting Max. He is good at his job but he doesn't have the greatest problem-solving skills. Got stuck, couldn't jump out…"

"So you picked up a huge dog that probably weighs more than me." She rolled her eyes again. "Next time, just get his front feet or something. Picking up half a dog is less likely to injure you than going whole dog."

"He's my dog. I don't like to see him scared or in pain. I'm a little sore, it's no big deal. I'd do it over again."

"Fine. Anyway, it doesn't look like it's more than muscle strain." She drizzled the oil on and spread it around, carefully avoiding looking at his face. Looking a man in the eye was like challenging him, and she wanted him to feel comfortable, not put on the spot. Besides, if he was feeling as vulnerable about this Jude situation as she knew he was, then he wouldn't want her seeing it. "What should we talk about?"

Anson shook his head minutely, but didn't answer right away. Not until she'd started working her thumbs into the corded muscle on his shoulder. "Your spirit quest." He grunted the words.

Ellory didn't particularly want to talk about that either, but a small amount of explanation could keep him from thinking she'd just gone down there for some excuse to 'do drugs with a shaman.'

"I needed to try and figure something out, and I believe we're our own best healers. Your mind and your heart can heal you if you let them. I didn't want to see a psychiatrist and tell her things I already know, and have her give me some pharmaceutical that might do more harm than good, a pill to dull and pollute. I wanted to get through it on my own."

"Did you?" he asked, and did honestly sound interested. She didn't hear the censure she'd expected. And to his credit he hadn't yet asked what her issue was, maintaining some respectful distance from that subject.

"Not all the way. But I figured out that I needed

to come home to get right. It gave me a starting point, and it also filled me with wonder for the universe… It's amazing that the earth gives us plants that allow for this kind of experience. I wish I understood better, but there's too much going on when you drink it. The shaman said it detaches your consciousness from your body, which sounds all woo-woo and like astral projection—something I'm not sure I buy. But I'm glad I went, despite having more questions than answers. Sometimes the biggest part of solving a problem is figuring out what the right question even is."

A soft pained sound escaped when her thumbs hit a particularly knotted area. He tried to cover it with words. "Did you go alone?"

"No. I went with my last boyfriend." She tried to ignore how final that sounded, like the last one she'd ever have and from here on out was a lifetime of loneliness. "He wanted to learn to hold those kinds of rituals so he could lead people in their own quests up here in the States, some retreat in Nevada he wants to work at. But I don't feel like his heart was in it for the right reasons. He was after money, not to help people. That's no kind of cause. So I left him there and came home. Been trying to work on my quest alone since I got back." She paused long enough for him to look up at her, establish fleeting eye contact, and asked, "Do you want to talk about Jude?"

Anson frowned. "There's nothing to say. He's still out there, and I'm getting a massage…"

"So you think you're letting him down."

"Of course I let him down." The admission came through gritted teeth, which either meant her thumbs were causing enough pain to make him grit his teeth or the situation was.

She stopped the deep kneading there and stepped forward until his head touched her chest. "Rest against me, I'm going to rub down your back, stretch those muscles out some. That will make it easier to work on your shoulder."

"That plan has me pushing my face into your breasts." He tilted his head back to look up at her as he said it, but his teeth stopped clenching, which she could only consider progress.

"Consider that a bonus." She smiled, "But if you ask for a happy ending when your shoulder is feeling better, I may punch you somewhere you wouldn't want me to punch you."

He smirked. "That could be anywhere. I'm not a fan of being punched."

"Just of punching. Which is how I know you're feeling worse than you let on."

He leaned forward, burying his face in the valley of her cleavage, and sighed. Still not wanting to talk about it.

"No motor-boating while you're down there either," she said, trying to draw him out of it a little. And it was easy to flirt with him. She hadn't seen a real smile from him yet and it surprised her how badly she wanted to.

Her teasing was rewarded with a little chuckle she felt a rumble through her chest to her belly, and his arms relaxed, elbows on his knees, his hands lightly cupping the outsides of her thighs. The innocent touch set off a wash of good tingles more powerful than his face on her chest. She'd long considered the back of the thighs an erogenous zone...

The tension in his spine lessened. Better. An even better sign that she'd be able to get him to smile later, when she could see it.

Another drizzle of oil and she pressed her thumbs into the muscle knotting the back of his neck, and stroked down along his spine, making little tight circles with the pads of her thumbs when she encountered a knottier area on his spine.

"How are you working on your quest?"

He still avoided the too-personal question, but kept her talking.

"Meditation. Exercise. Aromatherapy."

He laughed for real this time.

She was going to choke him. "Oh, hush, Doctor Man. You know that smell is one of the most powerful memory triggers?"

"So you're trying to recover a memory?" he asked, the chuckle fading from his voice.

"I don't know," she whispered, now that he'd started circling the subject she didn't really want to talk about. But lying was equally distasteful to her. She thought for a bit and tried to tell the truth while not exposing her tender underbelly. "This will probably sound all depressing, and I'm not depressed—I just haven't really been happy for a long time. Not truly happy or content. Doesn't matter what I do, even the highs I've gotten from volunteering and doing good things don't do much or last very long any more. It's started to feel like penance, and I don't know why." Which was part of it, but it still left her feeling vulnerable. She'd been hiding this from everyone.

Anson leaned back again, putting enough space between them to look her in the eyes.

Exposed. She felt exposed the way he looked at her, and aware of an unpleasant cold feeling in her chest. She looked away. "You want realigning."

Anson couldn't read her expression, but he knew a thing or two about living a penance-filled existence. There was such vulnerability to her honesty that it hit something inside him and made him want to help, to fix whatever was making her unhappy. She put on a good show. Had she not said those words to him, he might never have guessed.

"I need realigning," he repeated, no longer sure he was speaking of his spine.

"Right here." She pressed on the muscle that had seriously bunched up just below his shoulder blades, the pain proving her point. "T7 and T8 vertebrae. I can fix it if you get on the table."

She wanted to help him, and he'd let her. Maybe it would help her feel better too. "Fine, but I'm leaving the thermals on."

Her smile reappeared, though now he didn't know how real it was and how much was for show, even though he believed she wanted to help. She stepped back, pulling the towels with her and giving him room to move around. A pause to re-move his boots, then he stretched out face down on the padded vinyl table.

Before he could protest she swung one leg over his waist and he was caught by warm thighs and an overwhelming desire to roll over. Her small hands pressed into the muscle on either side of his spine, walking up and down a few steps until the vertebrae reseated with a loud crack.

Task done, she patted his back, climbed down, and left him thankful she couldn't see what the intimate position had done to him.

It wasn't Ellory's practice to molest people she had on her table, but the feel of his solid heat be-tween her legs made her breathless. She grit her teeth to keep her mouth shut, struggling to control the rapid breathing from the surge of hormones.

No matter that he'd spent the better part of ten minutes with his face pillowed on her breasts, he didn't seem bothered by her straddling, as she was. Although she wanted to talk to him about the situation that had put his hand going through a wall, maybe talking should wait… She continued working, tried to ignore the glide of the firm male flesh beneath her hands, and focused on the task.

By the time his arm was moving easily in the socket, the muscles worked to pliancy, he'd fallen asleep. She heard the slow, rhythmic breathing and ducked under the table to where his face perched in the padded donut-shaped headrest.

This happened a lot. Get someone to relax deeply enough, they fell asleep. And that was when they weren't exhausted and worried from all the hours spent in the horrid climate and stressful conditions. He needed sleep so she wouldn't wake him until he was needed.

Moving to the end of the bed, she pulled his socks off and swapped the oil for some lotion to rub into his tired feet, which was when she noticed them. Missing toes, two on one foot and one on another. He had no pinky toes. Her heart skipped.

Frostbite pain is monstrous.

His words came back to her, brought tears with

them that closed her throat. He knew that pain. No wonder…

She slowly bent his leg at the knee so she could see the top of his foot, and get a better look at the damage.

The scar extended far up the top of his foot, stretched out, pale and thin. An old scar. A very old scar, considering how far growth had caused it to migrate from his toes.

He'd been a child when it had happened.

CHAPTER FIVE

ANSON FELT SOMETHING touching his feet and snapped awake. Lifting and turning to look over his shoulder at the woman at his feet was harder, his movements sluggish and stiff. "God, what did you do to me?"

"Relaxed you." Ellory laid his leg back on the table and kept one hand on his foot. He wished she'd move away from them. "Your muscles will be a little slow to respond for a few minutes. You should drink a lot of water today too."

"Water?"

"Toxins."

He shook his head, not awake enough to run the mental obstacle course yet. Instead, he concentrated on lifting up and rolling over until he was sitting on the table.

"Toxins in your muscles get released with deep tissue massage. You should drink lots of water, flush them out. Or tomorrow you might have some mild flu-like symptoms."

"I thought the massage was supposed to make me feel better."

"How's your shoulder?"

Frowning, he tentatively lifted his arm and rolled it around in the socket to check. No catch. Sore still, but no catch meant no shooting pains, which was better than it had been.

He didn't answer her. Waking on the table he'd had no intention of climbing onto had left him feeling disgruntled and angry. And, pushy thing that she was, she'd had to get at his feet even though he'd told her they were fine...

"Frostbite pain is monstrous?" She pointed at the missing toes and looked up at his face.

He nodded. "You don't have to take care of my feet, you know. You can see there's no frostbite there."

"The scar has stretched and moved back from the toes."

He nodded again. She was already getting there. He'd just see how far she could take the logical path without his assistance.

"How old were you? Still in elementary school,

I'd say. Unless you still had really tiny feet in high school and they only recently exploded like peppermint in your herb garden."

Anson assumed that meant peppermint grew fast. The fastest way to get her to get off this subject was probably to answer her. "Yes." It was an answer.

And judging by the way her eyes grew damp, it was enough of one.

How the hell had this gotten so out of his control?

"Socks," she said suddenly, and sniffed, then popped into the changing room for a moment. When she returned it was with thick cotton socks, which she pulled apart, threading her thumbs into the toe of one and beginning to work it onto his right foot. "Your feet wanted different socks, and you shouldn't neglect your feet in this weather. Doubt you have any to change into. I usually put these on my patients when they have achy feet and want a wintergreen treatment. Thick warm socks while the rest of your body pains are getting worked on, it's nice."

Anson let her get one sock on, since she'd already started and he was moving with decided sluggishness, and then moved his feet out of her reach and held his hand out for the other sock. "You don't have to take care of me, Ellory."

"You're sad. I don't want you putting your fist through anything else."

"I'm not going to. I'm not sad. The fist through the wall did what I needed."

"Which was?"

"Pressure release. And it helped."

"Your anger maybe, but not your hand or your shoulder. And it didn't make you feel better about being inside and warm while Jude is out there. If you need to talk about it, you can talk. We're in this together, and you're helping me with our patient guests, so I want to help you too. Plus…" She stepped away from him and grabbed the sweater she'd discarded earlier, not finishing her sentence.

"Plus?"

"I don't know." She pulled the sweater down over her head, untangled her hair from the knot she'd twisted it into, and let it fall around her shoulders. "This."

Before he could figure out what she was up to, she'd stepped over to the table, wrapped her arms around his middle and squeezed. She cared, just as she had cared for Chelsea. But it felt good, gentle and warm, and gave him an overwhelming desire to bury his nose in the hair atop her head.

He resisted by tugging her back just enough that she looked up at him. The look in her eyes was anything but pity. Suddenly, all he wanted was to taste her. For a few seconds the world receded— he gave in to instinct and covered her mouth with his own. A small surprised sound tickled against his lips, but she tilted her head at the first brush of his tongue against her lips, opening her mouth to him.

Her scent might've been floral, but her mouth was sweet and fruity, just the barest hint of tartness that made him think of berries. Ripe, juicy, and summer-sweet.

And this was winter.

The disparity seeped through the subconscious need to consume her, and he lifted his head, reluctantly breaking the kiss.

Her dark brown eyes were even more heated than her pink cheeks looked. Those lush lips parted, as moist and inviting as her quick, shallow breaths.

* * *

"No, no…" Ellory whimpered, when she realized he was backing away. Every inch of her screamed for more. One kiss would not violate her Stupid Resolution.

Neither would two kisses.

And if he kissed her again now it could still count as one.

Her hands slid up his torso until scruffy beard tickled her palms and she could urge his mouth back to hers.

His tongue stroked into her mouth and she let go of his cheeks and wound her arms around his neck, sagging closer, resting against him, chest to chest.

Strong arms came around her, catching her when every thrust of his tongue made her knees threaten to buckle.

A kiss more intoxicating than a keg.

"This is not good," he whispered against her lips, just as she was about to start tearing his clothes off.

She was confident enough to call him on that one. "Liar. It's better than good."

So much better it was impossible for her brain

to begin comparing it to every other kiss in history, none of which had ever made her come close to losing control.

"Okay, not a good idea," he corrected, his voice holding a needy rasp that made her wonder how it'd feel against her ear with sexy whispers.

Which was definitely in the vicinity of violating her Stupid Resolution. "Yeah, maybe."

"Why are you still hugging me?"

She tilted her head and laid it on his good shoulder. "Because you need it. You're in pain and you're a good man. You're worried about…" She jerked her head back and looked up at him again, realization forming due to her mouth running wild again. Ruining everything.

"What?"

"You have a cause." She snatched her arms back and took two big steps back from the table.

"No, I don't."

"You're trying to make the world a better place," Ellory clarified, the realization making her exceedingly cranky.

"I am?"

"Yes, you rescue people from the winter! You

have a driving goal! You have a mission in life!"
Her stomach hurt. The man was definitely a danger to her Stupid Resolution, and her stupid quest
and her stupid everything…

"You are such a strange little thing…"

He didn't get it!

"You're my type!" She pointed a finger at him.
"And I'm not supposed to be dating!"

"I haven't asked you out, sweetheart."

And he didn't get it so much that he was joking around.

Ellory's cheeks had flamed to life when she'd
surged away from the table, like she had just
discovered she'd been kissing a big hairy spider.
"This isn't 1957. Women can ask men out."

His joking eased her enough that some of the
wariness left her eyes. She just seemed unrea-
sonably irritated by the fact that he spent half
the year helping people who got in trouble in the
snow. Especially considering her activities prior
to coming to this little special wintery haven had
all been aimed at helping people.

He shouldn't rile her up more. He should put
a lid on this situation, say whatever it was that

would make her relax. But she'd hugged him, she'd rubbed his feet, and then she'd kissed him back... She was so insistent on taking care of everyone, it was kind of nice to see that she had an unreasonable side.

Donning his best flirting smile, he popped his brows up a couple times. "Are you asking me out, Ellory?"

"You're not listening! I can't date you. I have a resolution!"

"You have a resolution, and I'm jeopardizing it by having a cause—which I really don't think I have."

"Yes, you do. And, *yes*. That's... Well, no..." She took a breath, her mouth screwing up in a way he was probably not supposed to find cute. "Having a cause is my type, but that's not the only part of my type." A few seconds passed as she looked to the side, brows pulled together, thinking, thinking... "Never mind. It's just that you're very good looking, and you smell like sex and chocolate...and Sunday morning. And now you have a mission to help others. For a second all that messed up my brain."

He could sympathize—his brain felt equally

scrambled. The difference was, he liked it. And he *really* shouldn't. Also, her description of his scent was probably the most outlandish and fantastic compliment he'd ever been given. That overt honesty charmed him as much as her manner of speaking amused him. He shouldn't be feeling this good. His job was unfinished and someone was out there waiting for the cavalry...

Remembering that took the spirit out of it for him.

"But the last piece is that you're like...a normal man."

"And you like weird men who want to be shamans." He filled in.

"I like men who would like me. And you aren't the kind of man who'd like me," she explained, and her declaration grew stronger with every version she repeated. "I'm not your type. So we would never date. You'd never date someone like me. So it's okay. It's okay! Everything is okay. Sorry. I don't process information quietly very well. It's kind of got to be out loud or it doesn't happen. I don't know why. Because I'm strange! Oh, thank all the gods."

Anson opened his mouth to ask what she was

going on to decide that she was not his type but a hurried request for help crackled through the radio, a voice he recognized.

He grabbed the radio, "Go ahead, Duncan." The most experienced EMT on the team, Duncan led it during the warm months, but stepped aside in the winter when Anson was around with his miracle dog.

One of the rescued was having trouble breathing. He got the room number where the patients had all been relocated, pulled his snow suit on—it was the only clothing he had with him—stuffed his feet into his shoes and took off out the door. While he talked, Ellory blew out the candles, turned off the lights and grabbed her keys.

Anson made a note to rile her up again later when the power went out…that could serve as hours of entertainment. Ask a question, make a statement, and then just watch her start spitting out random words that would eventually make sense.

Conventional wisdom did say that to learn to speak a foreign language fast, submersion was the key.

* * *

The regular fireplace suites were all situated in the same place on the floor plan for each level of the lodge, blocks of four stacked up for several floors.

The patient guests had been split into two groups and settled in side-by-side suites on the second floor—the closest to ground level, which was taken with communal and recreation areas, like the clinic and therapy rooms. With the frostbite to her toes and Anson's ban on Chelsea walking, she couldn't go anywhere without a wheelchair or being carried, so it made sense to locate them close to the ground in the event that the power went out and there were no elevators working. Easier to carry or roll her up one set of stairs than five.

Anson said the gibberish names of two different medicines as they passed the office, and where to look, then left her as he took the stairs to get to the person in distress.

She hadn't written down the medicines. She'd have to do that. This inventory thing could get out of hand fast, and she couldn't let Mira down. His kiss had done a brain scramble on her. So much

for resolutions. She hadn't even thought to protest when he'd gone all smoochy on her.

She was officially a weak-willed kiss pushover.

A kiss pushover who was obviously being given
more responsibility than she should be.

Ellory had never been an important part of
any medical team in a medical crisis before. The
knowledge that the rest of Anson's crew was
there helped her keep her cool, but her heart still
pounded. If she failed to live up to people's expectations now, someone could die.

One of the orange-clad rescuers stood in the
hallway, meeting her with an open door, which
she rushed through. Anson was already at the
window with Duncan and one of the patient
guests, who was clinging to the windowsill, his
head hanging out into the storm. Snow blew in
around him, but even above the roar of the wind
she could tell how labored his breathing was.

The group rescued consisted of two males and
two females, one other couple, and with Chelsea's
missing fiancé Jude still out in the wind, Chelsea
was sharing the suite with Nate, brother to the
other woman, and odd man out.

"He insists the cold air is easier to breathe,"

Duncan said, briefing Ellory on what was going on. They'd moved a chair to the sliding window so he could sit and breathe…but in Ellory's estimation it wasn't helping.

"Looks like that thing that happened with me last year," Duncan said, more to Anson than to her now.

How many years had Anson been doing this?

"Damage done to the respiratory system from the cold," Anson filled in, looking at Ellory's stash of medicines and supplies and then pointing to the inhaler she carried. "Pop the seals and shake it hard."

He listened to Nate's lungs again, leading him through breaths that were supposed to be deep but which ended up rasping and wheezing loudly.

"Had you been sick before you got here, Nate?" Anson asked, the concern in his eyes enough to worry Ellory. She prepped and shook the inhaler harder and faster.

When the man chose to nod rather than speak, she had a clue about how serious the situation was.

Questions flew about allergies, Nate answering

with shakes and nods of his head. He couldn't do anything but try to breathe.

Did he have any allergies? Yes. Food? No. Medicine? Yes.

In less than a minute Anson had gotten enough info to feel safe about giving the man the inhaler. He'd also started preparing some kind of injection.

"Nate, Duncan is going to pull you back into the room. I want you to breathe out as much as you can, Ellory is going to puff the inhaler by your mouth and you breathe it in deeply."

Anson looked between her and Duncan, making sure they knew their jobs. She liked it that he didn't repeat himself, didn't give them any extra instructions, just trusted them to handle things. It might not be the right call for every situation, but even she could handle an inhaler.

On the count of three, they all stepped in. While Duncan supported most of Nate's weight, Ellory watched him breathe out, holding his gaze. When he'd gotten out as much as he could, she gave him two puffs of the inhaler as he struggled to breathe in. Anson pushed Nate's sleeve up and injected something into the man's triceps, which he then rubbed to disperse.

His skin was very pale, maybe even a little bit blue—another skin color she could add to the shades that terrified her, right after the shade of Chelsea's poor toes.

Anson flipped the cap closed and handed the needle to Ellory, turned Nate's chair and helped settle him back into it…still near the window but not with his head hanging out.

Long terrible seconds ticked as Anson listened to his chest again, coaching him through the breaths as they slowly began to come easier.

She found herself breathing deeply, trying to breathe for the poor man, and noticed Anson doing the same thing. A quick look around the room confirmed it. They all breathed slowly, deeply, in unison, five other sets of lungs trying to do the work of one who struggled to breathe. All worried. All invested. All hoping it helped somehow. She felt part of something good, like she did on her missions, and it was probably silly since all she'd done was be the gofer and puff an inhaler. Still, it felt good.

As Nate's breathing stabilized, everyone else's

returned to normal… And that was what she had trouble letting go of. Not the drama and the fear of his fight for air but how for a few seconds all anyone had cared about was helping make Nate's world better. It didn't matter what kind of lifestyle these people led, they were still people. She didn't even have to wonder what her father would've wanted to happen in those seconds. He wouldn't have batted an eyelid if Nate had died. One less consumer, one less parasite devouring the planet while giving nothing back… She could almost hear the tirade.

Anson closed the window and came around, hand held out to Ellory. She put her hand in his, not thinking about what he wanted. It seemed like the natural thing to do. The warm squeeze of one hand, the other relieving her of the inhaler, cleared up what he wanted. Quickly, she let go of the medicine and Anson, and stepped back from the group.

"Respiratory infection?" she heard him ask Nate, who nodded. "If you're not completely over them, it's not a good idea to go out and exert yourself in the cold. Remember that."

CHAPTER SIX

FOR THE NEXT half-hour Ellory watched Anson listen to the lungs of the other patient guests, and then he made his crew breathe for him as well. He gave the same speech at least four times. Prolonged exposure to severe cold could damage nose, sinus, throat, and lungs when someone was healthy, let alone when they were getting over an infection or illness that had damaged them—as had been the case with Nate. She did very little but follow, watch, and listen.

Well, that and look the man over.

She wanted to kiss him again.

The world was coming apart at the seams, winter and wind and random acts of crazy nature, someone stuck out in it, someone's heart breaking, friends in anguish, and Ellory herself caught in a full-on lust-o-thon with the man who'd taken charge of keeping everyone alive.

The only thing saving her had been the dog.

He'd joined their tour of rooms as soon as they'd stumbled over him, and now he kept her company.

She spent most of the time crouched beside the big black fuzzball, petting him and whispering to keep herself occupied. Noting the changes in the rooms. She hadn't been in the fireplace suites in a long time. They'd been remodeled since she'd last been there. They were a blend of the new and the old, modern classy mixed with the comforting classics. But everything was secondary to the fireplaces.

Max was fascinated with her opinion on the décor and the superiority of the lobby fireplace to the ones in these rooms. They were top of the line, the logs looked every bit the real thing, and the hidden burners fed by gas and flames that wound through the wood…but it wasn't the same.

He agreed, wood definitely was better. "You're right. I should probably do some research and find out which one is the worst for the environment. But if we're using a hominess scale rather than the Scoville scale—or is that just about how hot peppers are?"

Real fire and all, but it didn't smell the same.

And it didn't talk to you, make comforting noises when the lights went out and the only thing to listen to was the wind.

Anson was saying something...talking treatment. More drugs, no doubt.

"What about the saunas?" Ellory snapped back into the conversation, standing in a room with just Anson, her buddy Max, and the last two members of his crew.

All of them looked at her.

"Steam is good for soothing the respiratory system." She shifted to one foot, half-afraid the people in the room were going to give her hell for even suggesting something natural compared to whatever came from a pharmacy and had the backing of the FDA. "It'd bring in moisture to what's been dried out. And we could put some therapeutic oils into the mist. Maybe some eucalyptus and rosemary...stuff that's anti-inflammatory and good for decongestion?"

Anson smiled at her but shook his head—nicely contradicting himself. "It's not a bad idea, the steam and oils actually sound quite good if you've got the quality oils for it. But moving them into the sauna might put more stress on their systems than would be beneficial. It can dehydrate and they're all probably more than a little dehydrated as it is." He looked at the other two. "Are we pushing liquids?"

A small conversation occurred about drinks and Ellory cut back in.

"We could just do it in a bowl and tent a towel over, a breathing treatment without getting everyone awkwardly naked together in the sauna. And I have good oils. Nothing synthetic, of course."

The lights flickering again had everyone looking up, breath held to see if they went out for good.

"Unless the power goes out and we can't effectively heat water," she muttered, more to herself than anyone else, and suddenly felt chilled by the prospect.

The power would go out. It wasn't even a question of whether or not it would happen, just when. With a little shiver she wrapped her arms around herself and rubbed her upper arms through the coat, which just wasn't pulling its weight heatwise. Though to be fair, it was probably impossible to keep her body temperature as high as she was used to having it with the clothing she had to choose from.

When the lights firmed up and stayed on, Anson continued his organization. "Get your helpers to start heating more water, and go find something warmer to wear. You're going to need it when the lights go out."

"I'm wearing the warmest clothes I have. I promise."

Anson rubbed his forehead, his words coming in short, clipped phrases. "Get everything set up. Water heated. Oils measured. My guys will run the treatments. Then meet me in the corridor. Be quick. I want to get this done before the power goes."

When had he gotten cranky? With the way things had turned out with Nate and the others, she'd have expected his mood to have improved, but in the last five minutes it somehow plummeted. Her clothes worried him that much? The loss of power?

"Enough for your crew and you?"

"Yes. Not me, but the crew."

"No one listened to your lungs," Ellory pointed out, feeling suddenly cranky herself. He hadn't let anyone look at his feet earlier, granted there hadn't been any *new* frostbite damage to look at, but he also had a problem he hadn't wanted them to see. Was he hiding something else by not letting anyone listen?

"Ellory." He waved a hand, cutting off her train of thought as well as the lecture that had been brewing, "See to it and meet me in the corridor when you're done."

With that, he was gone. And Max went with him.

Of course, Anson just stood in the hall and waited for her, like looming was his favorite pastime. Like she wasn't going to hurry, or maybe she was going to dilly-dally.

Ellory looked at him every time she passed, hurrying to and fro to gather the necessary ingredients for the steam bowls. Big metal bowls. Big fluffy towels. Eucalyptus, rosemary and lavender oils.

She couldn't read his scowl, he could be worrying about the power, but no doubt there was something else—something she'd done, the way his brooding and gorgeous eyes tracked her.

She hurried through her prep, counting drops into empty bowls, left instructions for the amount of boiling water to be added, then hurried to meet him before he had an aneurysm. "So, what's the plan?"

She could think of a good plan. A fun plan. A plan guaranteed to make him relax. A plan involving more kissing. A naked plan! But that would be a violation of her Stupid Resolution.

"To get you properly dressed," Anson answered. Of course he couldn't say Undressed—she'd told him about her Stupid Resolution.

"I told you, this is all I have to wear."

"What about Mira? Doesn't she have anything you could borrow?"

"Mira?" she said. "She's lean, toned and svelte. Have you looked at me, Anson?"

He took her hand and tugged her toward the stairwell. "I've looked plenty when you were ditching the sweater and wearing that...snug T-shirt." It sounded like he had some mix of pleasure and irritation at the memory, but at least she didn't have to actually say she was curvy like a mountain path, he got it. Mira's acceptable clothing wouldn't fit her.

"Where are we going?"

"Your room." He paused. "Where is your room?"

Bossy Man wouldn't be put off this until he saw it with his own eyes. "Fine. But you're not going to find anything more suitable." She tugged him toward the stairs up. "I'm not in the usual staff rooms. I have a guest room because I came late in the season and the staff rooms were already full."

She took the stairs at a jog, letting go of his hand so she could gather her skirts and avoid tripping and falling on her face. His shoulder was hurt. If she fell, no one was carrying her to safety.

Most of the employees being local was the reason there were so few of the staff on hand for this little adventure. The only ones here were actually living in the staff quarters—those folks stayed even when Mother Nature and Old Man Winter got into a spat.

And she was Mira's best friend, which meant she also probably got a nicer room than she might've otherwise—Mira knew how her living spaces always ended up. It just didn't bother her.

Over the last couple of hours she'd not only decided she wanted a vacation from her Stupid Resolution, she'd come to the conclusion that it was a good idea. Like eating a little bit of chocolate once in a while when dieting helped avoid going nuts one day and chewing your way through the donut counter at the bakery. Moderation was always a good thing, right?

She stopped just outside her door. If she took him in there, he'd know just how big a mess she'd become since coming home, and sex would really be off the table. "Anson, my room is messy. You could just trust me, you know."

"I can handle messy." He held out his free hand for her key card.

She could just say no. Put her foot down.

Make it seem like she was hiding something really nefarious in the room…

Or she could let him in and get it over with.

Since she'd come home her habits had grown out of control. But it wasn't until this second that she realized how out of control she'd become again. Until faced with the prospect of wanting to make a good impression, of having someone look into this intimate glimpse of her life, and the judgments that she knew would follow.

If nothing else, this trip into her obsessively

green existence would help her keep her Stupid Resolution. Find the bright side. Embrace optimism.

Be cranky later.

Find some company that sold environmentally friendly vibrators… That should've been her first purchase when she'd come up with this Stupid Resolution.

With a sigh she grabbed her badge, which pulled double duty as her room key, unlocked the door and stepped inside before turning to look at him. She stopped him following by putting her hand to his chest. "I don't have that many clothes. I could just bring them out to you here."

Anson looked her in the eye, and she looked away. Scared. Was she afraid to be alone with him in the room now? Not something Anson often experienced. People trusted him—which he could argue wasn't the smartest option given his track record—but it still bothered him that she looked afraid. "I'm not going to hurt you, Ellory. My hand hurts, my shoulder hurts…we're locked in here during a blizzard. It'd be extremely stupid for me to try something ugly right now."

She nodded, but the glance over her shoulder cleared it up for him. "When I said it was messy, I meant that I'm…I'm working on a problem I have."

"Your spirit quest?"

"Actually, no. That's something else. I think." She looked nervous again, then groaned. "God, how many problems do I have? I thought I'd gotten over this one! I was fine when I was away, but I come home and then I fall right back into a decades-old pattern that I hate."

Anson reached over and flicked on the lights, illuminating the room behind her, then steered her inside.

He had gone to college, so he'd lived with slovenly people before. When someone warned him their living space was messy, he usually had an idea what to expect.

That's not what he saw when he stepped into Ellory's room.

There were no clothes on the floor, no empty cups lying about or any real disorder that he could see.

But it was messy.

There were trays on the floor all around the

room with different kinds of tiny plants growing in them. "What are those?"

"Sprouts. Please don't step on them," she muttered, stepping around to the closet to wrench the door open, apparently in a hurry now to get this over with.

"I thought you didn't know if you were going to stay? You're already sprouting plants for…a garden?"

He followed her toward the closet, which required some careful stepping: She also had those rickety wooden drying racks located anywhere the air blew into the room from the central heating.

Her hands went up in unison, shrugging to the ceiling. "Eating. They're mostly alfalfa sprouts. I eat them a lot. They're great in salads and sandwiches and Mira likes them so I grow enough for both of us."

"I see." He wanted to ask why, the contradiction between the at times flighty but always proficient way she'd handled herself and the situation so far would've made him want to help even if he hadn't been undressing her with his eyes earlier. But it was another distraction. "Clothes?"

She reached into the closet and pulled out skirt after skirt after gauzy skirt, then wadded up something that looked even sheerer than what she was wearing…and threw it behind her.

"What was that?"

"Nothing!"

And yet her voice seemed to say, *I have candy I'm hiding behind my back that I took without asking.*

The whole thing took a comical turn and Anson found himself unable to keep from smiling at her. Definitely the type of woman every horny man wanted to play strip poker with—hot, and with an astounding lack of guile. "You know, I could reach around you and get it."

She grunted and held her hands up in front of her, which did not deter him at all.

"You don't need to see it."

"Is it a nightie?" He had no business asking that, but the bright peach blush warming her golden skin made him want to tease her more. And possibly convince her to model it.

"It's a belly-dancing outfit."

There was no way to contain the laugh that confession pulled from him. It was the last thing he'd expected her to say. "Do you have a tambourine in here too?"

"It's good exercise, and you can do it anywhere. And it's fun! And it doesn't require special equipment…"

"Just outfits."

"I made them so that doesn't count."

This flighty eco-princess thing was serious business to her. And the mix of sweet, eccentric and vulnerable worked for her. Ellory was definitely one of a kind—a bright spot in the storm.

"You're the first man I have ever met who thought it was funny that I belly-dance."

"I might change my mind if you want to belly-dance for me." He forgot all about the reason for dragging her off to her room. Now all he could think of was: the hot blonde hippie chick was also a belly-dancer.

It was like hitting the idiot frat boy lottery.

He really didn't deserve to see her belly-dance.

And that really wasn't going to stop him from trying.

"I'm sure you could convince me that it's not funny. I have a very open mind. And I like art."

The humor of the situation finally got through

to her and she laughed then shoved at his good shoulder. "You don't deserve to see it."

That struck a nerve, and his stomach felt hollow for the space of a couple of heartbeats before he realized that she didn't know what misery he'd caused in his life, so she had to have some meaning he didn't get. "Why not?"

"Because you think I'm an idiot." Her sing-song manner of telling him off made him feel guiltier.

Except that was one thing he was not guilty of. "I don't think you're an idiot."

"Then you think I'm a liar."

"No, I don't."

"You just dragged me up here to make sure that I didn't have anything more appropriate to wear after I told you several times that I was already making the best of things. So you have to think I'm either an idiot or a liar." She closed the closet door and crawled onto the bed again, her only route around him now that he'd blocked her from the closet and the rest of the room was some kind of cross between greenhouse and launderette.

"I don't think either of those things. I left you in charge of my patients, I trusted you to take care of them, and I completely approve of your breathing treatments. You also helped my shoulder, so I think you're probably very good at your job."

"Then why? If you wanted to come to my bedroom, God, Anson, all you would've had to do was say, Hey, want to get naked together? I've got this penis and I'm not doing anything with it right now. Want to see if it's a good fit!?"

Her terrible lines made him laugh again. "You do have the best pick-up lines I've ever heard." And would never in his life use, even if someone paid him and guaranteed that they would work. "You were right, though. I don't deserve to see you in that belly-dancing outfit...or to have any of the thoughts I'm having."

"Why not?" She tilted her head as she looked up at him, an intensity to her expression that made him want to tell her the truth.

"Because Jude is out there. I left him out there."

"So you punishing yourself makes him warmer?"

He knew how ridiculous it sounded, so he shrugged. It was the noncommittal kind of answer that usually got people to drop something when he didn't want to talk further.

"You know, I may not have much to show for

what I've done with my life so far—I don't have land, a house, a car. I don't even have a winter freakin' wardrobe." She hooked a finger in his belt loop, which kept him from stepping away, kept him focused on her.

"No. You're unconventional and not at all materialistic. I respect that."

"That's not what I'm getting at. I've been places. And I've seen suffering…" She stopped and swallowed, those expressive brown eyes letting him know she relived those bad memories when she recalled them. "I've learned that the people who survive, they're the ones who remember pretty quickly how to find joy in life. The others might keep living for a little while, but if they give in to the tragedy that has hit them, part of their soul dies. And soon enough they die too. Your body can't continue without your soul."

"I've heard the sayings. A burden shared is a burdened halved. All that. They're nice ideas… but do you expect me to go and tell those people jokes and make them laugh?"

"God, no. The last thing they needs is to think you're not taking this seriously. You have other resources, though. If you take joy where you can find it, that doesn't diminish your worry about Jude, or the unfounded guilt you're feeling because he's out there and you're not. It's okay for you to smile, and even if I protest about you teasing me about my belly-dancing, it's a good thing. And not only do you need it, but it's like an alternate fuel source. Good feelings can keep you going so you can actually get out there and look as long and hard as you need to in order to find him. You need it."

"Like I need hugs?" It was hard not to agree with her when she was standing right there, somehow making him feel better.

She nodded, and when he smiled rewarded him by lifting her sweater and the other layers she wore beneath it. His gaze dropped to the soft little tummy and he watched her slowly roll through the abs, activating one at a time to produce an undulating wave that…wasn't even a little bit funny but still made him feel good.

CHAPTER SEVEN

THE TOP OF his snow suit was still open, and while the branded insulated clothing she tried ever so hard not to covet might keep him warm, where it stood open down the front heat poured off him. She could probably go outside in her ridiculous clothes and survive the terrible winter if she cuddled up with the man.

For a second she remembered that the cold had hurt him, though. He wasn't invulnerable. In fact, she was increasingly certain that he was more vulnerable than he could even admit to himself.

She dropped her sweater and stepped forward, taking the opening given to slip her arms inside the suit with him and wrap them around his waist. Just one more hug. One more squeeze. One more pressing together of two bodies in need. He wouldn't mind…

It took Ellory tilting her head back and chancing a look up at him to make sure he didn't actually mind, though. His arms had come round her.

What she saw on his face made her belly flutter and her heart race—terrified and excited. He had that look, the one that split time equally between her eyes and her mouth. The man was going to kiss her again, thank all things holy. She wasn't out on this ledge by herself, the idea appealed to him too.

He had been to her room, had seen the disarray that went with her everywhere, had had a glimpse of the chaos she was currently swimming through, and he *still* wanted to kiss her.

Maybe.

He might be looking at her mouth but he was taking his sweet time about it.

Another look from eyes to mouth, and now the kind of frown someone only used when they were either concentrating or...

"If you have to try this hard to psych yourself up to kiss me, then forget it!" She let go, pulled her arms from the warmth inside his suit and made to step around him—using his belt loops again, though this time to keep from falling since he had her blocked in.

Before she got her first foot placed, his hands were in her hair, catching her head as he leaned down and covered her mouth with his own. His fingers, which had just a hint of roughness, massaged the back of her neck and sent goose bumps racing down her arms, neck and chest.

The first kiss had been good. An appetizer, a bite snuck from dessert before the main course. But this meeting of the mouths sent a tremor racing even more potent than the first streaking through her. If she bathed in champagne, Ellory couldn't imagine a more potent eruption of tingles dancing over her skin.

Instinctively, her fingers curled into the loops she'd snagged and she pulled closer, using him as an anchor.

She didn't even have the will to make excuses regarding her abandoned resolution. All she knew was the heady pleasure of soft lips contrasting with the light scrape of stubble, the strong arms that had wound around her, and heat.

He tasted even better than he smelled—better than anything she'd ever had in her mouth. Sex and chocolate, yes, sinful and decadent. But there was no hint of the indolence of Sunday morning now. Some time in the first heartbeats after his lips had touched hers, an urgency had taken them both.

His tongue stroked against hers, deep in her mouth, and her belly clenched. Desire licked through her, so strong it was all she could do not to tear the suit off him, get her hands back on that firm, glorious male flesh.

Firm and demanding, his hand slid under her sweater, seeking skin, fingers splaying across the small of her back. He felt it too.

She was ready to rip her clothes off, his clothes off…permanently swear off clothes! All she knew was that she'd never had a kiss bring her to life before. Make her forget her problems. More importantly, she'd never had a kiss turn her on without her actively trying to get turned on by it…and picturing kissing her daydream man in her head.

She opened her eyes, hoping to see that intention mirrored back at her, but the room was completely dark.

The power had gone out.

"Told you," she whispered, pulling his head

back down so that she could punctuate the words with a soft little kiss. "Lights went out, or I went blind."

He chuckled against her mouth, even though he knew he had to stop this. After one more kiss… Sliding his hand out from beneath her sweater—where it had no business being anyway—he wrapped his arms fully around her, crushing her soft body to him, soaking up every sensation, every piece of information he could before he gave up kissing her…

She wanted him as much as he wanted her, but she was a distraction…and a comfort he didn't deserve. It was unjust, at least right now. Maybe after the storm passed, after they had found the man and returned him to his loved ones alive… maybe he could pick up this raging attraction again. After he earned it.

He lifted his head, swallowed, and slid his hands on her shoulders so he could put her away from him a little bit. "How are we going to get out of here without stepping on your garden?"

His reason for coming to her room had been… "And the snow suit!" He cleared his throat, glad she couldn't see him yet. And that he didn't have to see her. The passion he'd glimpsed on her face the first time he'd given in to temptation and kissed her was almost too much to bear. The power being out now was a blessing. "Where's the snow suit?"

"Under the bed." She sighed the answer and crawled onto the bed at his side. "Stay there until I get the light." Apparently she'd picked up on his shifting mood. Which would make things easier.

Some clatter followed, and then the sound of cranking as she wound the eco-friendly lantern and cast the room in blue LED light. "Go sit down, I'll get it out. I'll bring it to the fireplace suites with us, but I am not wearing it unless we lose the fireplaces. It's really itchy and bulky and ugly."

Anson stepped over a few of the shallow sprout trays, made his way to a chair and sat to watch her crawl under the bed and carefully drag out a canvas duffel bag, somehow managing to keep from upsetting anything in this kooky ecosystem she'd built in her room.

When she righted herself, her cheeks glowed once more. He'd have said it was exertion that had caused it if she looked at him anywhere but the eyes.

Embarrassed.

That hadn't been his intention, though considering the way he'd dragged her to her room and questioned her ability to dress herself...okay, maybe he could understand the feeling. "It can't be that bad."

She shrugged and dragged it toward the door.

Rising from the safety of his chair, Anson took two big steps over the Ellory obstacle course until he stood in front of her, making her pause in her exit, and once more wrapping himself in that fruity floral cloud, and grabbed the massive duffel bag at their feet. "I'll carry it."

After dropping off Ellory's duffel in the suite next door, Anson entered the one saved for him and Max and found the big furry Newfoundland lying by the fire some thoughtful person had already lit, trying to keep ahead of the cold. His faithful companion stood and ran to meet him, tail wagging.

"So this is where you've been." He talked to his dog a lot. After he crouched and gave the big lover a good scratch, he found his way to the sofa and sat, leaving Max to return to the fire. As great as he was in the snow, he loved a fireplace.

Anson couldn't blame him, but after the trip to Ellory's room he knew one thing for certain— she gave out more heat than gas logs.

And he had no right to that heat.

On his last round to check on the rescued, Chelsea had shown him a picture of Jude. An engagement photo. Two smiling people with the future shining in their eyes…and he hadn't had the heart to ask her anything else about her missing fiancé.

He didn't need more motivation to want to find the man. So much of this situation echoed his own wintery nightmare. What he wouldn't have given for the fire in those days when he'd been so cold he hadn't wanted to move at all. The gaps between his snow suit and his skin had allowed the heat to build in pockets, and those pockets left the second he'd moved and the material had pulled tight.

All his hope had filled these small spaces, and all it had taken had been a muscle twitch to dispel it. Right now Jude was holding onto a thread of hope growing thinner and more brittle with every frigid breath he'd drawn since this morning.

A knock at the door brought him back to the present. Max lifted his big shaggy head and looked at the door. A couple of sniffs of the air and the search dog's big tail began beating the carpet.

No calls had come through on the radio, so it wasn't an emergency. He'd like to ignore it. Go to sleep. God, he was tired…

Anson peeled himself from the sofa and made his way to the door. Max beat him there.

"I see how it is." He ruffled Max's ears and pushed him back so the door could swing open.

Ellory stood behind a stack of sprout trays, arms straining to carry them. Her warm brown eyes met his over the spring-green shoots, and she smiled. He couldn't see her smile, but he saw the apples of her cheeks bunch and merriment in her eyes.

She kicked the duffel bag he recognized, and the stuffed thing flopped through his doorway to land on his feet. Heavy. Big. It took up as much room as at least two of his suits. Max sniffed the hell out of it.

"I need to bunk with you," she said, the strain from carrying the trays down several flights of stairs and long corridors showing in her voice.

Anson grabbed the bag and hurled it further into the room, then grabbed the edges of the bottom tray to relieve her of her portable garden.

"No. Your shoulder is hurt. Just move." She refused to let go, but since the way had been cleared she stepped forward to come in.

"No," he repeated back to her, and lifted, forcing her to let go. Once they were in the room, he placed the trays on the counter. Which was when he noticed two other bags swinging from her shoulder. She didn't travel light...

She closed the door and dropped her bags.

"Let me guess," he said, looking at the sprouts. "You're here because you changed your mind about that belly dance."

"Nope." Ellory looked the tiniest bit guilty then. "I can't bring myself to have a wasteful fire all to myself. And no one else would understand if I brought the sprouts and crashed in their pad. They'll be ruined if I leave them in my unheated room. I don't really know anyone else well enough to include them in...this. And...well, you kissed me. You like me. I like you." Max barked at her. She hadn't paid him any attention yet, and he wasn't having it.

"And I like you too, Maxie." She caught his front paws in the chest and roughed up his ears with the kind of affection usually reserved for someone's own pet. "I'm sorry I left you out. Go and tell Anson you want me to sleep over! Go tell him!" She pointed at Anson and Max dutifully ran to him, tail wagging hard enough to clear a table, tongue lolling out of his mouth. Happy panting.

"What about your resolution?"

"I'm not asking you to marry me, Anson. I'm not even asking you to curl my toes and make me forget that my enviro-OCD is out of control again, or whatever else is wrong with me that made me think coming home would fix it." Edging around the sofa, she dropped her other bags on the floor and took a seat there in front of the fire. "I just want to share space. And maybe I'd like to spend some time around a wild man who puts his fist through walls...and his dog."

As soon as she said the word "dog" Max came and flopped down on her, then rolled so he was on his back and his head propped on her thigh, all but demanding belly rubs. Anson briefly considered doing the same thing to her other thigh, but having it known that his dog had better moves than he did was just too much for his ego to handle today.

"Max clearly wants you to stay." Anson wanted her to stay too, he just wasn't into admitting that right now.

"We should move the bed over by the fire." Ellory didn't sit yet, but Anson did.

"It's not that cold in here. For people dressed better. You should put on your suit."

During the hour since Anson had kissed her lips and made her feel like she was drowning in champagne Ellory had devised a plan.

Or, well, she'd *un*-devised part of her plan. The whole point of her resolution had been to remove distraction and give herself the attention she'd normally pay to a relationship, so she could work on herself. Figure out what was wrong with her. Figure out what she wanted to do with her life. Traveling was getting old. She wanted to settle down, but she didn't want to lose her ideals in order to build a life.

Tearing off Anson's clothes and dragging him to bed wouldn't change any of that. It wouldn't solve her problems. It wouldn't make them worse. If anything, it made her more acutely aware of the fact that they were waiting for her. And they would still be waiting for her when the skies cleared and the power came back on, and Anson was no longer stranded here with her.

"Or we could go to bed and be warm under the blankets. I brought my quilt, it's really warm and snuggly." Temptation lit his eyes, but was chased out by that deep scowl she'd come to loathe. "Or you could go to sleep by yourself and I will go spend time with Mira and the patient guests. She's come down, by the way. You've got some free time to sleep if you want it. You look like you need it, and if you aren't into chasing away demons for the next few hours in the manner we'd both enjoy, then you should sleep."

She thought a second and added before he could protest, "Better now than when the storm clears and you have to go back out after Jude."

"No argument here." He untied his boots, kicked

them off and stripped out of the suit as he walked to the bed.

Ellory watched until he was under the blankets in his thermals, at which point Max gave up his spot by the fire and went to curl up on Anson's feet on top of the fluffy duvet.

After she spent some time making sure everyone got fed, she'd get some sleep too.

On the couch. She'd already made enough moves on the man. The next move was his.

Ellory awoke after a long night of lumpy sleep on the couch, burrowed beneath her quilt with her head propped on one of the cushions and Max panting in her face.

"Good that you woke up. I think Max was about to wash your face. With his tongue," Anson said from where he sat, using her duffel stuffed with the snow suit from hell like a beanbag chair in front of the fire.

The dog's tongue was exactly the last thing she wanted on her face this morning. But after the way the night had gone, and the fact that she was sleeping on the couch when she'd much rather have been sleeping beside big warm Anson…well, Ellory didn't wake up feeling chipper.

Rolling over so she faced the couch back, she pulled the quilt over her head to block out the smell of dog mouth and ignored both of them.

When the power had gone out, Mira couldn't be kept out of things any more, so in theory Ellory didn't have anything to do this morning. No duties to perform, nothing to organize. And as guilty as it made her feel to be glad about that, she figured she'd probably handled things as well as she could for as long as she could. Two straight days of organizing and keeping everything under control was too much responsibility and decision-making for her.

Besides that, yesterday had felt like it had been weeks long.

And today still felt like yesterday, however that worked out.

The smell of food filtered through the quilt now that Max wasn't breathing on her face. Eggs. He was making eggs somehow. Could you cook with gas logs?

She closed her eyes tighter and tried to ignore the scent.

Her stomach growled.

"The storm is still going." Anson spoke again, apparently not satisfied with her attempt to cocoon herself away from all contact. "But the kitchen staff brought up breakfast. Scrambled eggs and toast."

So he hadn't cooked.

But someone else had. Someone she wasn't mad at. Someone whose food she could eat.

She was mad at Anson? The realization startled her enough to bring her up out of her quilt.

She took inventory. A frown, but nothing teary going on in the eye department. A desire to hide out, sleep some more and guilt him over his great sleep... A martyr complex about her own sleep, which had been anything but restful.

She *was* mad at Anson.

Weird. She rarely ever got mad at anyone. So rarely she couldn't remember the last time she'd gotten angry about anything. When someone disappointed her, she usually just got sad, and then moved on.

No matter that she'd playfully threatened to punch him yesterday, she had never engaged in any sort of violence. But now? She might be able to do something aggressive. Like throw something at him. Pelt him with scrambled eggs.

Well, she just wouldn't think about him. Do whatever needed doing. Ignore him.

Mira probably needed help anyway, and she'd have to sleep at some point…so maybe Ellory wasn't off the hook anyhow.

She crawled out from beneath the quilt, stood and shook it out, then carefully folded it before draping over the back of the couch.

"Not speaking to me today?"

No. Not speaking to him today. She pretended he was talking to the dog and went about getting her stuff together. She dug a fresh skirt from her bag, and then another… As they weren't as substantial as yesterday's barely substantial skirt, she pulled them on over the unflattering long thermal underwear she'd been wearing since yesterday. She hadn't brought any clothes-drying racks with her, naturally. And there was no hot shower. No sunshine. Because winter sucked, and winter in Colorado sucked even more.

She pulled on a fresh sweater, yanked from out of her collar the braid she'd worked her long hair into before sleeping, and went to wash up.

However they'd been cooked, she'd eat the damned eggs. Whatever realizations she might've come to last night seemed much harder to follow through with this morning. It took concentrated effort not to wonder where the eggs were sourced—or any of the other ingredients.

They were probably from chickens full of hormones, just like she'd felt she was since the grave doctor had grumbled into her life: full of hormones.

Sighing, she grabbed a handful of sprouts from the bin from the third-day ready-to-eats, rinsed them and sat at the table, her back to Anson.

This would teach her not to prepare ahead of time for these types of situations. With the predictable nature of the power to the lodge, she should have been making and storing granola bars and trail mix, dehydrating fruit—just doing something besides growing sprouts...

Max came around and rested his chin on her knee, giving her big sad eyes.

Okay, half of a sandwich for her and half for Max. She pulled the sprouts off his half and handed it to the dog, who took the sandwich and ran off to eat it.

"He has already eaten."

Well, he'd just eat more.

Ellory took a bite of her sandwich in silence.

"Did I do something to tick you off?"

Yes. Probably. She just wasn't sure what it was.

Maybe it was the rejection. Or the double kiss and run. Or the couch.

"I'll take the couch tonight." He pulled out the other chair at the table and sat where she couldn't ignore him as effectively.

She finished with her current bite before even trying to answer. It'd be the height of irony to be killed by foods that she usually avoided because they were bad for you. "Don't bother. I'll find another room." There, she was even proud that she managed to speak in a completely level and natural-sounding voice.

Anson gave a low whistle, leaning back in his chair until it tilted on the back legs, and linked his hands behind his head. "You really are mad."

CHAPTER EIGHT

MAX CAME BACK for more and Anson set himself back upright, snapped his fingers and pointed to the fire, and the dog obediently went to lie down.

Ellory took a big bite of her terrible sandwich and considered giving the rest to the dog.

"Did something happen that I'm not aware of?"

"Probably."

"Did I talk in my sleep?"

"I don't know, I didn't spend the whole night watching you sleep," she snapped, getting more and more worked up as he pumped her for information—obviously not feeling the same courtesy to refrain from badgering her that she extended to him. "I might be struggling with my compulsiveness about my carbon footprint and about what I eat, but I'm not a psychopath, a sociopath, or any other path that I can't think of right now."

"Did you have a bad dream?"

Not deterred.

Why was he not deterred? Did people yell at him all the time? Was this how he liked to communicate?! "I don't know. I don't think so. I don't think I slept enough to dream anything of significance." Ellory pushed the plate away and went to get more sprouts. Eating the sprouts didn't feel like punishment.

"The couch is uncomfortable." He offered another incorrect guess.

"More comfortable than the ground," she muttered between fresh, crunchy bites.

"What does that mean?"

"It means I sleep on the ground all the time. So if I can learn to do that, I should be able to sleep on a cushy couch in front of a fire. Well, a fake fire. The hissing sound it makes…and this place smells like gas to me all the time, even though I know the gas can't be leaking—the fire would burn it up."

"So the gas kept you awake?"

Like he could fix that if she confirmed it bothered her. Ellory thought about doing what he liked to do—go silent and brood or punch things—but talking about the fireplace was better than talking about the real problems. "Yes. And some other stuff."

"What stuff?"

"I really don't want to talk to you about it. You've seen enough bad things about me, and to give you credit you're handling it better than most normal people would."

"I haven't seen any bad stuff about you," Anson said softly, shrugging. "You keep saying that I'm normal. The insinuation being you're not normal."

"Yep, that's the insinuation." She stopped there, shrugged and shook her head. The only word that came to her was even more negative than usual. Broken. She felt broken, and with no idea how to fix herself. No idea how to learn to be content...

"Quirky. Free-spirited," he filled in when she didn't finish the thought.

Ellory grunted, stuffed some more sprouts into her mouth and resisted the urge to throw them at him. She might not have anything remotely natural to eat if she gave in to the urge to smash them in his face. "Stop sucking up."

"Something must have changed in the night."

But somehow, as they talked, she got less irritated with him. Even though she didn't want to tell him anything. Which was when it became clear. "I came home for a reason, because I have to figure out what is wrong with me and fix it. Instead, I had some kind of compulsive relapse, and I told you about it! I told you more than I've told anyone else about it. I haven't told anyone what's going on with me. I told Mira that I needed to spend time working on myself, but not why. But I've been open and all that with you. I hoped that you would open up to me too. But you didn't. You won't even admit that you are upset about anything. I can't help you if you won't even talk to me at all."

Anson righted the angle of his chair and linked his hands on the table, his eyes staying fixed on her even if she couldn't read them right now. "What makes you think you can be of any help to me? Or that I need help in the first place?"

"Please," she intoned, running a little water into a cup so she could water her sprouts and at least be busy doing something while he gave her the third degree. "I'm on a quest too, even if I'm not currently 'doing drugs with a shaman in the jungle.' I can recognize a fellow traveler when I see one. You have the look. You're searching for something…"

"The only thing I'm looking for is for the storm to pass so I can actually go out and search for that man."

She said the man's name even if she knew how it made Anson react. "Jude." Immature of her to say it, but she couldn't help herself.

"Yes, Jude." He bit the name at her, his voice finally rising from the calm, detached doctor voice he'd been using on her. "And I will be fine again once I can go out there and find him."

"Fine. You're fine. You're perfect and great. You punch the wall every time it storms." She poured the rest of the water into the sink and ate another pinch of sprouts for good measure.

"Do you feel better?"

"No, of course I don't feel better! You can't make me *un*-mad at you by basically saying I'm dumb for being concerned about you." She shook her head, eyes rolling. He was just being obtuse on purpose, she knew he was smarter than this.

Max stood up in front the fire. Now that voices had been thoroughly raised, he was becoming upset. Ellory watched him rise up to sniff Anson's face, and when satisfied he was okay come to sniff her. "Down." She lowered her voice and petted his head then shoved him gently but firmly to the floor.

When she spoke again, she kept her voice level, for the sake of the dog. "For the record, I'm not mad about the couch, it was a symptom. Not mad about the food. Not the weather. Not the hole in the wall. I'm mad that I shared something with you that I haven't shared with anyone—even my best friend. I thought that we were bonded or something after yesterday. But I felt lonelier last night than I think I ever have while in the same room with someone. So, yes, I'm not feeling my sunny self. I'm disgruntled and I'm going to find somewhere else to stay. I shouldn't have invited myself to begin with. I'll be back for my stuff."

She stepped behind the chair she'd been sitting in and scooted it back under the table—keeping things as tidy as she could was the only way to deal with the amount of clutter she traveled with. Then she slung on her coat, dug into her bag for clean socks and her boots, and left barefooted. She'd put her shoes on in the hallway, or some-where else she couldn't feel him watching her, glowering at her. Somewhere Max didn't follow her around, looking worried.

So he didn't want to sleep with her. So what? Lots of men didn't want to sleep her. And he didn't want to talk about how he felt about Jude or how he'd lost his toes. That was his personal business. Her focusing on his emotional well-being was probably just her using him as an excuse not to focus on her own emotional well-being anyway. And a danger to her Stupid Resolution. The heart of her resolution was about fixing herself…and there was no difference in the level of distraction between dating a man and fixing him.

She didn't want to tell him anything about her past, though, which was stranger than anything else. She was like an open book, or she tried to be. People asked her questions, she answered them. She didn't lie. She didn't conceal. Not usually. She had flaws and she embraced them or tried to change them, but she didn't hide them. Until now. Until this problem.

She hadn't been lying to Anson when she'd said she wanted to be content, she wanted to be happy. She just didn't know what exactly was standing in her way.

All she did know after this morning was that she needed to talk about it. As much as she didn't want to give her best friend something heavy to carry when she was supposed to be enjoying new love bliss with Sex Machine, she had to tell Mira as much as she knew.

She could only hope that putting the words together would give her access to the information her conscious mind had trouble getting at.

Ellory made her way through the circuit of rooms, knocking on doors, checking on staff, and worked her way back to the patient guests' rooms, with Chelsea's room her last stop. Mira was there, the two of them in front of the fire, talking in low tones to avoid waking Nate.

She snagged a chair from the table and as quietly as she could moved it over to where the two women sat, forcing as much chipper as would be appropriate, and making her greetings in whispers, then added to Mira, "Your relief is awake, so you can go off duty and get some rest again. Where's Jack?"

"I can stay a little longer." Mira gave her a long look, no doubt picking up on her fake chipper.

"Jack has already gone back up to the suite, you just missed him."

"I wasn't really looking for him," Ellory admitted, "Just thought you might like to get back to him." And then she focused on Chelsea. "How are you this morning? Is there anything I can do for you?"

The small woman shook her head. "I'm hanging tough, as Jude likes to say. Dr. Dupris and I were talking about how we knew we were in love."

"Oh." Another conversation that she couldn't really participate in, though at least this time it wasn't because she was being excluded.

She just didn't have anything to add. She had never been in love and she'd never claimed to have been in love, but who kept track of that kind of thing? Would Mira put it together? Should she be ashamed of that? Was that something she should admit?

Now she'd found something else she didn't want to tell anyone. All this hiding had to stop.

The other two repeated their tales for her. The way his voice could make her heart flutter, the way her belly flipped when he looked at her, spending the whole weekend in bed together and refusing to even answer the phone and be apart for a minute... Stories full of smiles and epiphanies, details burned into their memories.

Having shown her the way to tell this particular kind of story, Chelsea fixed her with a hopeful smile, expecting a similar one.

Ellory could only shrug. "I don't have a story like that."

When both women looked a little sorry for her, she added, "I have sexy stories, but this is probably not the time for those. I also have lots of feel-good stories about weighing malnourished children when they were finally starting to put on weight. I can tell you about the sounds of the rain forest at night and stories about food I stopped asking for details on...because it might involve bugs. They're good stories, just not the 'I knew I loved him when' sort."

Mira was a wonderful doctor, she knew just when to push and when to hold the line, and although the smile she gave Ellory said she would get it out of her at some point, she gave her a pass because of the people around.

Mira tried to change the subject, and Ellory wanted to let her, but she had joined their conversation for a reason and it seemed like as good a moment as any.

"Mir, I haven't been entirely honest with you, hiding something…which is probably making it worse."

Mira glanced at Chelsea and then looked back at Ellory. "Do you want to go somewhere else to talk?"

There was a suggestion in her tone, and Ellory realized only then that it might give Chelsea a bad impression. "Chelsea's already seen some of it," Ellory murmured, and then looked to see if the woman wanted them to go somewhere else.

"What did I see?"

"I apologized for the cocoa," Ellory said softly, then refocused on Mira. "You know how a few years ago my attempts to…be environmentally responsible got a little…out of control?"

Mira nodded, a thoughtful frown on her features. She summed it up in one word. "Preservatives?"

She meant the cocoa. Ellory nodded. "And, well, the sprouts. The clothes washing in the bathtub and drying on racks in my room, never using the lights or…well, the electricity in any way I have control over…"

"Is that why you wanted to come home?"

Mira sounded confused, which Ellory couldn't blame her for. She ran on instinct more than anything else, probably because she had such a hard time identifying what she actually felt at any particular time, let alone being able to explain it.

"That was the spirit quest."

"Right." She nodded, and like a good friend and doctor she asked questions, gathered information to make a treatment plan. "How long has it been bad?"

"Mostly since I came back. I didn't know exactly what I was working on at the time of my spirit quest. I just was looking for…contentment, and an indication of what I was supposed to be doing with my life. The only answer I got was that I needed to go home…so home I came."

A knock at the door preceded Anson and Max strolling in, there to check in, no doubt. Her stomach bottomed out, and she looked everywhere but at his eyes.

"I just wanted you to know, in case I've been extra…eccentric lately." She focused back on the two women, and Max came to nose at her hand until she petted him. "But we can talk later. I'm sure Dr. Graves wants to…do his rounds."

With everyone in a holding pattern until the storm let up and no emergencies currently happening, Anson and Max had nothing to do. Except wonder about Ellory. And why she'd fled upon his arrival. How could she be that mad at him?

"Actually, if you don't need me, I have something to discuss with—" Anson didn't get through the statement before Mira waved him off.

Time to put an end to this quarrel, whatever it was.

By the time he got Max out the door, Ellory was nowhere in sight. He hit the stairs on the chance that she'd gone back to do that moving she'd threatened him with.

How had she gotten so wrapped up in his life—in his mind—in twenty-four hours?

When he'd lain down last night, it hadn't been with the intention of hurting her, or making her sleep on the couch. Hell, he hadn't even meant to sleep so long, just a nap to recharge. But his body had had other ideas.

He and Max caught up with her and followed a few steps behind, all the way to their shared suite and in behind her. She went for her bags first.

"Put those down." Anson gestured to the couch. "We don't want you going anywhere, Max and I. You want to talk. Let's talk."

"Is this some kind of trick? Don't think I won't move just because you make it sound like Max needs me." She blotted her eyes with her sleeve, turning her face away from him as she did. Crying? What had escalated things to crying level?

"No trick." He closed the door behind him and decided to give her a moment to breathe. "Let's move the mattress in front of the fire, like you wanted." Physical things were easier to take care of, and the action gave him time to think.

Moving the couch and furniture out of the way was easy enough. By the time he'd moved to the bed she'd joined him, and together they lugged the unwieldy thing to the cleared spot in front of the fire.

Max thought it had been put there for him, naturally, and ran over to lie down in the middle.

"No, Max. Go lie down." Anson ushered the big dog off the bed, then bent to unfasten his boots so he could shed the snow suit and be a little more comfortable on the floor bed. It also gave him an excuse to get under the quilt with her once she'd settled with it. "What were you three talking about?"

"I already talked a bunch."

"Okay. Me first." He pulled her against his side and anchored an arm around her waist. "When I was ten I was lost on the big mountain for several days with my mother during a storm," he said without preamble, since it seemed like the easiest way to start this story.

She looked up at him, her eyes going unfocused beneath frowning golden brows. Not really looking at him—that was the look of someone searching her memory. Did she remember hearing the story? Had he become a tale told to frighten local children into right outdoor behavior? It was something he never talked about, so the idea had never occurred to him.

"Did you hear about that?"

She shook her head. "Maybe…I'm not sure."

His relief surprised him.

"We crawled under a ledge to get out of the snow. The ledge wasn't small, but it was very close to the ground. Too close for us to do much besides lie there on our backs and wait for the storm to pass. It took a long time. By the time it was past I was drifting in and out of consciousness. My mother…she died."

Ellory looked down to where his legs disappeared beneath the blankets and with one hand she found his closest foot. By chance it happened to be the one with the most damage. The one she'd been looking at in the massage room before he'd kissed her.

He felt her hand curl around the remaining toes and squeeze, but she didn't say anything. She just rubbed his disfigured foot, which he'd really rather she not touch at all—he didn't like anyone touching his feet.

Before he could stop her, she'd snagged the top edge of the sock and pulled it down and off his foot. Anson had to work not to say anything or stop her. Not that she was going to say or do something cruel, but he just didn't like how exposed it made him feel to open up about this stuff, to let someone see the mark of his shame.

She wouldn't know that part. He hadn't told her everything.

"You touch everyone," he said as her hand curled over the decades-old scar.

"Yes. I touch everyone." She finally spoke as she caressed his foot and leaned her head on his shoulder. "People need to be touched in order to be healthy. Touching heals and…" She started to say something else but stopped short.

He'd finally started to understand most of what she said without asking for clarification, but when she left off thoughts entirely, he still needed help. "And what?"

The woman was like an exotic creature he had no chance of understanding if he didn't ask all the questions that other people would leave alone.

"That's how I express love."

That sounded like a declaration. Only it couldn't be, they barely knew one another. And she touched everyone. Compassion. She meant compassion.

"I can't imagine how alone they're all feeling right now, even if they're in it together. Especially Chelsea. The man she loves is still out there because he wanted to save her. I want her to know that I feel for her and that there are people here who want to help her through this if she wants the help," Ellory murmured, but she didn't sound like herself. "Sometimes it's harder for someone to hear words than just to offer your touch and presence for them."

Like she was touching him now. It was still all about how he was doing, making him feel connected to someone and better, whether or not he deserved her compassion.

"It's good. I had teachers in school who made a point of telling some…well, a good number of the students to touch their patients."

"All book, no heart?"

"Something like that."

She may be all heart. Based on their fight earlier, he knew she wasn't just sad for him and the patients. She was struggling too. He held back telling her more, and pretended it was in case he should need to barter the information with her later, because he really needed to know why she was crying. "Why were you crying earlier?"

Her eyes warmed again, giving Ellory warning that tears were imminent. She laughed. "So annoying, you can just mention tears and they spring right back up." A sniff and she swiped her eyes again, mentally cursing her lack of control.

"Only when you've stopped crying because

you're avoiding what upset you." The gentleness in his voice helped. At least it pushed away the embarrassment she felt as the result of tearing up.

"Mira and Chelsea were talking about being in love," Ellory began, trying to find words that fit what she felt so she'd actually know what she was thinking. "These moments of insight when they knew they were in love…"

Anson's arm came around her again and gave a squeeze—encouragement to talk, not that she needed encouragement, she just needed words. It was sweet anyway.

"Started thinking about someone you lost?"

If only that were the case…

"No. I realized I never loved any of the men I have been with. Not one of them. I never had that realization of love." She couldn't look at him. The confession sounded terrible enough to her without seeing disgust or something worse in his mossy green eyes. "Which is horrible, I know. And makes me sound like a—"

He shushed her. "It doesn't make you sound like anything."

"Not something bad? Because you'd think I would've loved some of them, they were all perfect for me in some way. We were…" She started to claim they were just alike, but the words sounded false. "We had a lot of the same ideas and beliefs. And they were always doing something good. And they taught me…"

Anson let her work through things at her own pace. She tended to work through things out loud, and he suffered her pauses with patience she only recognized when she'd fallen into her thoughts long enough to make him prompt her. "Elle?"

"I know why I've fallen apart since I came home."

He could hear the disgust in her voice, and it was all Anson could do to keep from dragging the information from her.

"What did they teach you?"

"They taught me their habits. We usually lived someplace where simplicity was the only option, and I just did whatever they did. If they had fruit salad in the morning, that became my routine too."

The sigh that came from her was so forlorn his first instinct was to change the subject. Don't make her dig that deep—he hadn't dug that deep for her earlier. The difference was he knew how he felt, he knew what had happened, he knew what he'd done. He'd examined it all so many times the memories barely made him feel anything any more—except shame.

But it was clear her process was one of discovery. Not something to be shut down. Clean out the wound so it can heal.

"Whose habits are you following now?"

"My father's. And they keep invading what I do. Like when I was apologizing for the cocoa. That was a habit he gave me."

"How so?"

"When I failed to follow the rules in some fashion, his favorite punishment was a diet of junk food. Because if I behaved like the rest of the parasites on earth, I should eat what they did so at least I'd not live very long. Some kids got grounded, I got fast food, the greasier and more processed the better."

Anson felt his mouth fall open. The psychological warfare of that made it horrifying. Other kids would rejoice to eat candy and snack foods, but if she'd been raised believing that they would kill her—and that her father wanted to her to die young because she didn't live up to his expectations… That was a special kind of twisted.

"There are a bunch of ways to live the kind of life I need to live, but I come here and I fall into this pattern of extremes. It's ridiculous that the place I love more than anywhere on this earth turns me into a basket case. I want to stay, but I don't know how I can if I can't get control of this. Figure out how else to be. Relax my rules. Or actually just figure out what *my rules* really are. Right now, central heat feels like a gateway drug! It's not even something I can control here, but it's like some slippery slope that's going to make me give up my beliefs or compromise my ideals. So I push to the other extreme, as hard as I can, and…"

Her words died, but he knew it for what it was now: where her epiphanies dried up. She burrowed closer to him and he tightened his arm, for once uncertain of what to do, or even to say to help her.

Max finally picked up on the tension in the room and invited himself to the bed with them, where he could plop his big heavy head onto where their knees met.

Ellory took it as a request to be petted, and obliged him, comforting the dog who wanted to comfort her. It was exactly what they were doing—a cycle of comforting and no one fixing anything.

"Change one thing you're doing," Anson said, the only solution he could come up with that didn't involve putting his fist through something living and infinitely more deserving than the drywall.

"What thing?"

"I don't know. The sprouts. Get rid of the sprouts." It was the first thought that came to him.

"But I like the sprouts."

A gust of wind rattled the window, timely and a reminder. "Get a new snow suit, one you'll actually wear." There was a ski shop downstairs. She could do that immediately, which would give him some peace of mind.

"We're not dating, but how is that any different than me just adopting your habits?"

"It's not just my habit. My habit is an orange reflective snow suit. A regular suit is the habit of everyone who hits the slopes during a Colorado winter." He strenuously avoided using the word 'normal.' She didn't need those kinds of comparisons right now. "You get a suit so you'll be better protected, and you'll be changing something small. And I'll do something for you in return. I'll do…spirit quest stuff. Just no drugs."

"Ugh, stop calling it a drug. It's a natural decoction," she grunted, pulling back so she could look him in the eye. "You'll do spirit quest stuff if I get a new snow suit?"

"That's what I said." It might not solve anything, but it was something that they could do that might let her feel like she was helping him too, which balanced the margins. She didn't need to know his margins could never actually be balanced.

"You could also look for a job once the storm passes. I know a few centers I could recommend you to."

"I don't know if I want to work at a center. Regimented schedules are hard for me."

"Okay. Then make some plan. Come up with what your ideal situation would be if you decided to stick around." He wanted her to stick around, God help him.

She laid her head back down on his shoulder and resumed stroking Max's snout so he'd stop making big sad eyes at them both. "What are you going to do for upholding your end?"

"You tell me. Where do we start?"

"Meditation."

The rest of the day passed at a lazy pace. No emergencies dragged them out of their meditation, and Anson only really left when it was time for him to make another round to check on everyone. Just because no one was in a state of life-threatening duress it didn't mean he slacked off on his duties. They all ate together, and Ellory managed to make something that didn't send her into an OCD tailspin. Mira provided a key and Anson helped her pick out a snow suit from the shop—not too big but big enough to hold in some heat—and set his mind at ease.

When watching the fire got old, they spent time in front of the window, watching the snow swirl and blow.

And he held her hand. All the time. When they were alone in the room, Anson held her hand. She always had known that touch healed, reminded you that you were part of something bigger, a way to share strength. She'd always believed those things, even if she didn't feel it as deeply as she wanted to.

But as they sat by the fire, saying nothing, his support flowed into her and carried away the loneliness she'd been feeling since…always.

As night came, Ellory felt content for the first time in a long time. It probably wouldn't last. Maybe not even the night, but it was a start—like glimpsing the end of your journey while still on the mountaintop, with days of hard travel still to make.

With their thermals still on, they stretched out for the night, Anson's big body behind her, matching her bend for bend, his arm around her waist. "Wake me up if you have bad dreams," she said over her shoulder, then settled down to the smile-inducing feeling of his nose burrowing into her hair.

"I should get it out of the way. Braid it."

"Don't you dare," he mumbled, his arms tightening.

CHAPTER NINE

ANSON LET HIS eyes close and tried to make his body relax. She felt too good, she smelled too good—especially in this position, where he got the sweet, natural scent of her beneath the long sun-kissed honey locks he'd like to wrap himself up in.

So he'd managed to avoid kissing her today, which didn't mean much considering where they'd ended up anyway. People who weren't already feeling intimate didn't cuddle. Two people who just happened to be sharing a bed and who didn't want more than that…they lay with as big a gap as they could between them.

"This is a joke," Ellory muttered, pulling thoughts right out of his mind. "I can't sleep like this. If you don't want me, if you don't want to want me, or whatever, then I should sleep on the couch."

"You're not sleeping on the couch." And, by

God, neither was he. Anson sighed into her hair, keeping his arms around her.

Ellory looked over her shoulder at him. "You know what I would be doing right now if we *were* dating and you were being this big of a brat?"

"I'm not being a brat."

She snorted and then beneath his hands he felt her tummy do that roll thing again, which pushed his thoughts further down that path they should not travel.

"You're the brat."

She rolled her tummy again. "Did you know there are a whole bunch of ways to move your tummy and your hips? It's about controlling muscles, not just the abs but accentuating the movement of the hips and the curve from waist to hip."

"You're playing dirty."

"I haven't even begun to play dirty." She laughed and then did something with her hips that rubbed that firm round little tush against his groin. In an instant he was hard, and just like that he stopped caring whether or not he deserved her attention and the amazing womanly body pressed against him. He had it. If Fate was making a mistake, then Fate would be to blame.

Except…

"I don't have condoms."

"I do!" She scrambled out of his reach and leaned off the mattress, one hand on the floor so the other could reach her bag and drag it over. The position gave him the best view of her backside, and before this second he'd have never said thermal underwear was sexy.

"Your thermals are too snug. They're supposed to be loose to keep you warm…"

"Shhh." She flung condoms at him, and then started peeling those thermals off, starting with the top.

The room was fairly warm, but as the shirt whisked over her head, he could see that she was a little chilled. The shirt landed on the floor and she was about to strip right out of everything else, her thumbs in the waistband of her leggings, when he grabbed her by the hips and dragged her back to him on the bed.

"I get to take those off." After he kissed her. After he got to explore the gorgeous flesh he'd already been granted the pleasure of.

* * *

As he slid her beneath him, Ellory reached for the hem of his shirt, pulling it over his head. While her confidence might be hit or miss in other areas of her life, one thing she'd never had a compunction about was nudity—her own body or the nude bodies of others. With the kind of life she led, there were a great many communal activities, and her actual between-missions job was massaging frequently naked bodies…

Since the minute Anson had yelled at her and dragged her inside from the cold, she'd been trying not to think naughty thoughts about him. Seemed like forever had passed since then. She might not have the most accurate concept of time, but she was pretty sure that her massage of his shoulder and back had lasted three whole years. And in the intervening years since she'd had him on her table—yesterday—she'd missed the sight of him.

As soon as the thermal top was off, she did what she'd been itching to do since the start and ran her hands over his chest, lightly scratching her fingernails through the whorls of dark hair that danced over his glorious torso.

"You're beautiful." She hadn't meant to say that, but the smile he gave her made her glad it had slipped out…so glad she almost said it again. Instead, what came out was, "Let's take off your pants!"

Anson laughed again and pinned her hands above her head, levering himself over until his deliciously manly chest and belly flattened to her own.

But one kiss, and the playfulness was gone. The third kiss was the charm. In the space of a single heartbeat her thoughts turned as chaotic as her body became needy.

Heat.

Hunger.

And on the horizon the likelihood of hurt. Nothing good could come of this. It was not dating. It wasn't a relationship. It wasn't anything except the moment.

Forbidden fruit, the allure of what could never be.

His tongue dipped into her mouth and he let go of her hands so he could lean off her again and remove her bottoms, every inch of flesh exposed burning with awareness.

Under any other circumstances she couldn't have him and he would never want her. But right now he needed someone to lighten his load and she needed to feel connected to someone—that's what they'd be to each other.

Being the leader meant keeping up appearances to those who looked to him for something. All Ellory could think to look to him for right now was some relief. And maybe being able to save him from something, since she couldn't freaking figure out how to save her own damned self.

She was just the life raft.

And that was okay because under any other circumstances she wouldn't…well, she probably just wouldn't want to want him. The idea of actually not wanting him was so far removed from what she felt right now that she couldn't even really picture it.

He kissed and licked his way down her chest, with detours to kiss and suck. When his teeth scraped her nipple she thought she'd come apart, the growing tension the only thing that held her broken pieces together.

Even knowing this man was a recipe for betraying herself and her way of life. A gorgeous man with a cause, and standing. And who knew what else? His lifestyle was a complete unknown. He could be the picture of everything she'd hate. But with the way he made her feel she had to consider that he'd still be someone she'd change herself for. Her mother had changed for the love of her father. Even as a child, Ellory had understood that.

She'd tried to change and make her father love her too—but he still didn't. He never could, just like Anson never could. She'd never been able to fit into her father's world, and she couldn't fit into Anson's. The best she could manage was a short stay in this twilight zone version of it. The lodge was a deserted island, a bubble away from the rest of the world.

So he wasn't really a violation of her resolution. This wasn't dating. It was sex.

The desire she felt for him might leave her feeling like a virgin on the cusp, but it was still just sex. Just sex. Much-needed sex, sure, but still… Just. Sex.

As he kissed and licked his way over her belly to her breasts, the extreme appetite she'd developed for him took over. Lifting her legs, she hooked her big toes into the waistband of his thermal pants and dragged them down, causing his erection to spring free.

Her toe tracked over a scar on his thigh, which she registered…something to ask about later, when stopping wouldn't kill her.

Everywhere his mouth touched her skin became heated. Something she'd never experienced with her past lovers—this need. She ached to the point that the whole thing was becoming unpleasant.

One hand shot to the side, where she thought he'd dropped the foil packages, and half felt, half banged around on the floor. "Condom…condom." She panted the word. When he lifted to look at her, there was a question in his eyes.

"I don't doubt you'll remember. And this isn't a date. And neither of us thinks so, right?" And with her brain functioning at half-power she added, "I'm not supposed to have babies."

He reached for one of the condoms she'd pelted him with, bit into the foil, placed it over the head of his shaft and unrolled it with one stroking fist. The bruised knuckles even thrilled her. There was something incredibly erotic about watching his muscled arm complete that motion, and she was never so happy to have massaged someone in her life—gods only knew how this would go if his shoulder still hurt like it had.

His hands fell onto the mattress at either side of her and he lowered himself until they were pressed together again, his sheathed heat between her legs, though he made no move to enter her yet. "Why aren't you supposed to have babies?" The words were an effort for him to speak, every one carrying an edge of tension and urgency.

Had she told him that? "Uh. Well…because I'm not supposed to be alive."

She grabbed his head and tugged his mouth back to hers, needing his kisses like she needed air. He pulled back long enough to look at her, a question on his handsome, scruffy, three-day bearded face, but to her relief he didn't ask. Instead, he reached between them and glided the head of his erection over the little nub begging for his attention, and then drove into her with a single thrust.

She arched, lifting her hips from the bed, pushing against him in such blatant wantonness she kind of shocked herself, but he wasn't moving yet—just holding her, pinned by his big body and the frowning concentration in his eyes.

"Don't look like that," she muttered, wiggling her hips again to try and spur him on. "What's wrong?"

"You will explain yourself to me after we're done." He gritted the words through clenched teeth.

Ellory groaned then slid her hands down his back to squeeze his clenched butt as he held himself motionless inside her.

"Say it."

"No." Already flushed and wanting, the heat that stole over her face now was of a very different sort: anger. She was mad at him again. "This is cruel."

"Say you will explain it when we're done or we're done now."

"No."

He began pulling away. The madman meant it!

"*Fine*," she growled, now really wanting to hit him. "I'll tell you but this is blackmail."

The savage smile he gave her made her want to hit him even more, but he pressed forward, filling her again and then establishing a rhythm she was too thankful for to remember to be angry.

Bracing her feet against the bed, she lifted her hips to push at him and he took the hint, rolling with her, letting her be on top. There would be no more withholding anything from her if she was in control.

She'd just stay sitting up, it was a little bit of distance because he was a big hunky jerk and he didn't deserve the full-length loving.

But within a few measly heartbeats she'd leaned down to kiss him again, and his arms locked back around her waist, chaining her to him so tightly that she could feel the instant their heartbeats synchronized. Not every beat, but as they moved it became obvious to her that they were meant to be there together—two heartbeats that overlapped for short intervals that gradually became one thunderous, unified hammering as they built to a climax so fierce and pure she could have cried.

Ellory believed in fate, and that sometimes things were meant to be. She and Anson, here in this moment, was bigger than her pitiful needs, desires, or resolutions. Their hearts beat together.

She could only pray hers kept beating when they came apart again.

* * *

The curtains had been drawn before they'd gone to sleep, the extra layer of wind protection also keeping it mostly dark in the room.

So it wasn't the light that woke Ellory. It was the foreign sound of the fireplace clicking off. That hadn't happened since they'd moved into the suite. The wind had been blowing hard enough that the thermostat in the fireplace fought constantly with the wind to keep the room warm.

But not Ellory. She had a big warm man behind her, wrapping her in heat, and a big warm dog on her feet, keeping them warm.

Max lifted his head to look at the fireplace, which gave her an opening. She rolled to face the sleeping doctor, who had at some point put his shirt back on. She found the hem and slid her hands inside over the firm male flesh and the crisp tickle of hair against her palms.

Anson awoke to the feeling of Ellory pushing his shirt up. His chest was bare by the time his mind cleared and he lifted his arms enough to let her push the warm material over his head.

"I need skin. Why did you put these back on?"

she grumbled, her voice just a little bit raspy from sleep. Sexy.

Just like that, he woke up.

She nudged him until he rolled to his back and she rolled with him, straddling his hips in a position that reminded him of last night's activities and made his body respond—intentions forming.

Wiggling around a little, when she was satisfied with the bare chest-to-chest position, her head turned to press her cheek into his shoulder and her nose up under his chin. "Just so you know, we can have morning sex and it still doesn't mean we're dating. We're still not dating, we're just comforting each other."

"So your resolution is intact?"

"Mmm-hmm."

He grinned, his hands stroking over her bare back, having not really had the time to luxuriate in her body when they'd been together before.

The sound of silence cut through the sexy haze settling over his brain. No hissing from the fireplace.

No wind.

No wind!

Light reflected up onto the ceiling in a pink band above the curtains.

"The storm…" He rolled her off him immediately and stood up to look out the window. Deep snow, at least five feet, had been dumped on them, but it was calm now and reflected the soft pink hue of sunrise.

Ellory joined him at the window, pulling her thermals back on. He didn't look, he was still waiting for his body to catch up with his brain and give up on the idea of sex so soon after it had become ready for it.

"It's over?" she asked.

"We can go back out."

Ellory looked toward the brand-new snowsuit laid out like a deflated person-shaped balloon on the sofa. She'd already purchased the thing, not wearing it would be even more wasteful than wearing it. Plus, if she wanted to go out with the team and help look for Jude—which she really did—she'd have to put it on.

While Anson was on the radio, waking everyone up, Ellory got dressed in her new gear.

"You have to eat something before you go out there."

"The kitchen staff are going to make breakfast now," he said, turning to look at her by the door. "Where are you going?"

"I was going to talk to Mira for a minute before we go out." She said the words casually, hoping he wouldn't pick up on her meaning until she was actually out with him and he couldn't...

"You're not going."

Do that...

"I want to go." He should know how badly she wanted to go considering her getting dressed in the new—and worrisomely awesome—snow suit. "I want to help."

"I know you do." He sighed, scrubbing a hand over his face. "But Mira is going to need your help. Chelsea isn't going to want to leave, but with the snow past, you can get her and Nate to the hospital. Have Mira call for a chopper or maybe another crew to come up. Do they have a snow coach or something here? Multi-passenger? Preferably enclosed. I'd rather keep Nate out of the cold wind as much as possible and Chelsea can't wear her boots while her toes are swollen."

Ellory frowned. "Mira's a doctor too, you know. She can handle this stuff. Plus she knows how things work here and I don't. If I come with you, I can maybe get places you couldn't. I'm smaller."

"How big is Jude?"

Okay, she didn't know how big Jude was. He could be Anson-sized for all she knew. "Probably bigger than me."

"It's dangerous out there. I don't want to have to worry about you too."

"If I stay with you—"

"Ellory? I'm not having your life on my hands too. That's how it is out there. I have to find the one who is lost and keep my crew and Max safe. That's seven lives on my shoulders. I'm not adding to that weight with one more person who won't be of any help and who I don't need."

She flinched and hurried out the door before he could say something else negative. No, she didn't know what she could do, but it was doing something. An extra pair of eyes would be helpful. When she was just here, just waiting for them to return, it had been bad enough when she hadn't even known him.

* * *

Even when someone was as on the ball as Mira was, it took time to ready the snow carriage to transport patients down the mountain. If they waited until tomorrow the workmen would've had time to inspect the cables leading from the resort down to the town, but just jumping into an aerial carriage and hoping for the best would've been colossally stupid after the couple days they'd had.

Since Mira was doing the organizing, she waited with Chelsea. "How are you doing?" She dragged a chair up to Chelsea's wheelchair and sat, offering a hand should the woman need some support.

"Bad," she admitted, and then took Ellory's hand. "I know that I need to go to the hospital, and Nate needs to go too—we probably all need checking over, but I want to stay. Even with the power situation as it is, I just want to be here for the instant that they find him."

Her hand felt dry and tight, still chapped and rough from her time in the storm. Spotting a bottle of lotion across the room, Ellory stood and went to get it. She made a conscious decision not to check the chemicals, poured some into her hands and set about rubbing it into Chelsea's hands, working the muscles as she went.

"I pray that they find him today, but if they don't, we'll make sure you get regular updates."

"Regular updates?" Mira said from behind her, having entered quietly. "Absolutely. I've got my cell and I will call your hospital room several times a day to keep you up to date." She gestured to what Ellory was doing and asked, "Almost done?"

"Yes, just rubbing the lotion in. Are we ready to go?"

"They're out plowing the lot now and someone shoveled a path to the snow carriage, so we can go as soon as we're ready."

Anson had a plan, but he didn't have a good feeling about it. Normally, out on the mountainside, doing his job, he felt peace. There was purpose to it, the extreme focus and need to push himself cleared his mind of anything else. Even the cold air he breathed exhilarated him.

Today every breath burned, both going in and out. Which was how he knew it was in his head and not him coming down with whatever Nate had been ignoring for his ski vacation.

There was no thrill from zipping around the mountainside on his snowmobile, though he usually loved it. Snowmobiles triggered avalanches easily, and because the day before the snow front had arrived had been sunny and warmer than usual, it had weakened the snow supporting the thick, deadly mantle they were all riding around on. Even without them making any mistakes or pushing any limits, that layer of snow could slip at any time.

Six people on his crew meant he had enough to split up in to three teams and work on the buddy system, driving far enough apart that if the ground started to slip it was less likely that both searchers would be swept away in the snow, and all were wearing locator beacons in case the worst happened. Even Max had one on his collar.

Anson looked behind him in the mirror again and caught sight of his buddy, and then Max's big head filling up the rear view, panting in that way that looked like a smile.

Having the Newfoundland with an insanely talented nose made their searching easier.

Anson stopped outside South Mine, got one of Jude's shirts from a plastic bag he carried, and opened Max's cage. By the time his search buddy reached him, Max was already snuffling the shirt and taking off for the mine. Both rescuers grabbed their lights and followed him inside, but the dog didn't stay.

Jude wasn't in there.

He sniffed in a circle in the entrance, and then headed back outside to sniff the air, looking for an air trail to follow.

The wind was blowing from the northwest—the direction of the lodge—and Max got nothing. No excited yips that would indicate he'd found a trail.

Anson pulled his radio off his belt and called it in. "Search team one at South Mine. It's clear."

The radio crackled and it became immediately clear that Ellory was still considering herself part of the search, even if he hadn't let her come out.

"What does that mean? Where are you going now? Did Max pick up which way to go from there?"

She didn't even know how to use a radio properly.

"No, he didn't. Would've been hard considering the storm, hard winds and deep snow."

"Oh."

He heard the disappointment in her tone. And since he'd already disappointed her once today he added, "If he found a scent, it would probably mean Jude was outside in the snow, and that would be bad news. The other teams are going by foot through the woods to try and pick up his trail where we couldn't search. And to hit the cave between. We're going northeast."

"But that's away from the lodge."

"I know. I'll call when we've reached the next stop."

He ended the communication and stashed his radio again, getting Max back into his cage to go.

He'd probably given her false hope. If the other two teams didn't find Jude where the snowmobiles had been unable to travel, it was unlikely they'd find him alive. Everything else was outside the direction he should have traveled, which was why they were heading off in the wrong direction.

That's where he and his mother had gotten lost: Down the wrong side of the mountain.

CHAPTER TEN

TWILIGHT HAD ENDED thirty-seven minutes ago, which meant it was officially dark. So dark Ellory could probably see the Milky Way if she looked long enough.

They were supposed to stop searching when it got dark. It was a rule. The other two teams that made up Anson's crew had returned to the lodge, but he and Marks? Still. Not. Back.

Ellory didn't need to ask why they weren't back yet. Anson was pushing it to the last possible moment in order to find the missing skier. Or past the last possible minute...

Because they hadn't found even a trace of Jude. Yet. Yet, yet, yet. She mentally scolded herself for her pessimistic thinking. As angry as she'd gotten while waiting for them to return—and being mad at Anson again just underscored the fact that they were incompatible—she knew Anson would be beating himself up more than she could ever stand to do.

With the snow that had fallen the risk of avalanche was incredibly high. The teams had managed to trigger two different small slides today without getting trapped in them, which was why they didn't bring in a helicopter for air searching yet. They'd been lucky that the slides had happened in areas where there weren't caves or mines where Jude could be hiding.

Headlights bouncing off the blue night-time snow told Ellory they were back, and no one else would have to say boo to him about being out there after dark. She was going to confront his handsome and well-toned ass, and she didn't even like the idea of it.

In her new suit—which she loved even more after a couple weeks of Colorado winter in equatorial clothing, she stayed inside the breezeway leading to the lobby, opening the outer doors from the inside when Max got there, and then again when the bipeds caught up.

"It's dark," she said to Anson, who stepped past her and into the lobby, making a beeline for the fire she'd kept stoked for them. "You are supposed to be here before it's dark. When it's still light out. To travel safely...*more* safely. Two slides! Two in one day."

She put a bowl of warmed water down on the floor for the dog then grabbed two big mugs of cocoa she'd been keeping warm and forced them on both men. "Drink this. And say you will be back earlier tomorrow."

Anson took the cocoa thankfully and drank it down fast enough that she once again felt compelled to apologize for giving him food with preservatives in it. Maybe they'd preserve him longer if he got trapped in a freaking slide tomorrow. "We checked in."

Sure, but after dark, and the only way that would've comforted her was if he'd also kept up a steady stream of running chatter on the radio while they'd been driving back, so she'd know from second to second that he'd still been alive. "Not recently."

"Elle, I can't talk and drive at the same time. It's treacherous out there."

"Yes. Yes, it is." She puffed and took a seat, making herself calm down before she actually did yell at him. He looked haggard, worse than he had that first time she'd seen him, and he'd been grappling with the idea that he had lost his first person on the mountain overnight. And put his fist through the wall.

"Tomorrow more crews with their own dogs will be here. Mira called up everyone she could think of when we were getting Chelsea and Nate down to the hospital. We passed power crews working on the poles and the power should be back on tonight or tomorrow," she informed him. "Two of her toes had sprung big blisters this morning, so they've confirmed that she has stage-two frostbite on two of her toes. But they've got a treatment plan and said it's very unlikely that she'll lose them."

He nodded, still grim but happier to hear some good news. Because the window where they could hope to find Jude alive was rapidly diminishing. She couldn't even think about what that would do to him.

"The original rooms in the lodge, the first ones built, still have water heaters that run on natural gas. Mira showed me today and we all had baths. You can have a hot shower to warm up. I'll take you to the rooms. But the rooms are pretty cold.

No fireplaces there so dry, dress and get back to your real room so you don't get pneumonia or something."

She led them to the rooms they'd been using, steering Anson toward one and leaving Marks for the other, pointing out that fresh towels had been put on the bed for him. And repeating her warning that he not dawdle.

"Are you okay?" she said to Anson, as they and the dog stepped into the room. She'd lit candles in there earlier. They'd been burning since the first staff member had gone to shower, so the room was not nearly as chilly as she'd expected. Max hopped onto the bed and lay down.

Anson sighed and shook his head. The admission surprised her. "I don't think he's alive. And what a coward I am. I didn't want to come back here and have to tell Chelsea. The others... I know they're all close. I can tell the other two..."

"They all went down together. No one wanted to wait here."

"Because I can't find him?"

Ellory stepped over and helped him with his suit, knowing how stiff and useless your fingers got when you'd been in the cold too long. "No, because they want to be with Chelsea and Nate. And Mira and I both promised them that we would contact them if the situation changed, and Mira is taking lead on contacting them several times a day anyway, just so they expect to get updates and all that. Waiting is murder."

"You have no idea."

She wanted to ask, but the wound seemed too raw right now. Instead, she just continued helping him undress. And once he was in the shower she undressed too and joined him under the spray. It was dark so she couldn't see what he was feeling by looking at his face. The best she could do was distract and comfort him.

If she was honest, that wasn't all it was. She needed a little comfort too.

By the end of the second day of searching the power had come back on, returning them to the twentieth century, but the broadband was still out, making rejoining the twenty-first century still a goal. Anson and Ellory remained in the fire-place suite they'd been using for the extra heat the gas logs provided. And she didn't feel at all bad about the carbon—not because she was adopting the habit of her current boyfriend, he wasn't her boyfriend, but he needed the heat. He needed it, and that was enough to keep her from focusing on the negative.

By the end of the fifth day, no matter what she tried she couldn't get him warm when he came in.

The hearty and thick lentil stew she'd made didn't warm him.

The showers he took were so hot they left him a vigorous shade of pink, but still didn't manage to cut through the ice that had settled in his core. When he stepped out of the steamy shower or bath he got cold again.

Worst of all—the sex failed to heat him up too.

Bleak, fast, and over too soon, Ellory felt blistered by the haunted look in his eyes, even at climax. She'd have sworn he didn't want her there with him at all if every night he didn't wrap himself around her on the mattress that still rested before the perpetually burning fire, and burrow beneath the thick duvet and her quilt.

Even when the heat he surrounded himself with made him sweaty and miserable, he still shook when he slept. He still said he was cold.

The sex was supposed to help him sleep, but it

didn't. He remained stiff behind her, except for the constant low rumble of shaking that seemed to come from his chest and shoulders.

They both avoided mentioning the elephant in the room: everyone's worry about how long they would be able to search for Jude, and when would it be called off or considered pointless?

Putting the thought out of her mind, she rolled to face him, her hand coming to cup his cheek and force his eyes to open. "You have to relax."

"I'm trying." He licked his lips. "I know I should be sleeping so I can be my best tomorrow, but I just really want to get back out there right now. I'm not even sleepy."

"Do you want a massage?"

He shook his head.

She didn't offer sex again, it hadn't worked the first time and with his head as screwed up as it was right now he didn't need to venture into anything adventurous and kinky in search of relaxation.

"Meditate with me."

"Elle, I can't concentrate right now."

"You don't have to concentrate." She pulled away from him, though it took effort—he didn't want to let go. "I'm not going far." The words were ones she might've said to comfort a child. Grabbing the quilt from on top of the duvet, she shook it out. "Sit, legs crossed."

His arms loosened.

To his credit, Anson didn't sigh. He didn't roll his eyes. He sat up and did as she asked.

Ellory wrapped the quilt around his back to keep him warm and then climbed onto his lap, wrapping her legs around his.

"Is this some kind of sex meditation?" he asked, wrapping his arms around her waist as she settled against him. The tremor he was unable to stop made it feel vaguely like cuddling a big manly vibrator.

A shake of her head. "No. It's much simpler than that." She combed her fingers through the hair at his temples and kept his face facing forward. "All I want you to do is look me in the eyes. Watch the light of the fire, and just be. You don't have to do anything. I don't expect anything from you. It's not so hard to look at me, is it?"

"It's incredibly easy to look at you," he breathed back, but his brows were still pinched, like he was concentrating. "But how is this meditating?"

"It's supposed to make you feel safe…and connected. Do you feel safe?"

He gave her one of those smiles that contradicted his pinched brows.

"How about connected?"

"I feel connected."

That one she believed, but he needed to relax his brow if he had any hope of this working. She pressed one thumb between his brows and gave that muscle a firm rub until it relaxed, ran him through some breathing techniques and then settled her arms around his shoulders.

Her neck relaxed a little, causing her head to tilt to one side, and stared deep into deep green and hazel eyes, saddened at the bleakness there.

He mirrored the action, keeping their eyes aligned.

She kept her voice gentle, wanting nothing more than to soothe. "We're sharing energy. It's like physics. Entangled particles. We will just sit and be together, share breath, share heat, share touch. You will look into me, and I will look into you. And when our particles are good and entangled, no matter where you are on the mountain, doing this terrible job that needs to be done, you can share my peace and hope when your well has run dry, and I can share your burden."

He swallowed, but he didn't argue. She half expected him to declare the exercise stupid and pointless, but surprisingly his arms relaxed until they were more looped around her than holding her.

If there was one thing Ellory knew how to do, it was relax. She could cast off her conscious mind with astonishing ease, having learned long ago how to escape into her imagination.

Pulse and respiration slowed, relaxation extending from her body to her eyes. The focus went past the firelight dancing in his mossy eyes, and images started to emerge. First blurry, then crisp. A home in green fields, babies with eyes like the forest, and fuzzy black puppies. She saw the green fading from his eyes, the dark fringe of his lashes turn sparse and grey, and love that grew strong.

She saw everything she'd always said she never wanted, and knew it for what it was: the biggest lie of her life. The bond she felt with him, the aching need, that was love. She loved him. This was that moment that Mira and Chelsea had been describing, where her heart swelled and… She remembered she couldn't have that future. She couldn't have him, but she couldn't even begin to understand how she would ever be strong enough to walk away from it.

Anson shook her.

Something cold and wet splashed on her chest, and she realized she was crying. Her breath came in broken hiccups and she let go of his shoulders. "I can't do this." Her having some kind of a break-down wasn't the purge he needed to start heal-ing. It was hers. How many purges did she have to have to reach the bottom?

"Why? What just happened?" His voice firmed with intention, focus, and he kept his arms locked around her waist. "What are you afraid I'm going to see?"

"I don't know." She pulled back hard, and turned to crawl off him and away. Just get away.

He let her go, sounding bewildered but not fol-lowing. "You do know. What's wrong?"

"I don't know," she repeated, and only stopped once she reached the farthest corner of the mat-tress, her back to him, on her knees, struggling to calm herself.

This was supposed to be for him. Metaphorical, a way of releasing tension, not anything real. If this was how he felt...

She gulped the air, smelling the sharp ping of the natural gas from the fireplace and focusing on that smell, using it to clear her head. This was supposed to be about him, not about her...

"Talk. You said you put things together in words. Talk." His words came from right behind her, and his arms came around her waist again, pulling her back to his chest and then into his lap as he sat. "You're not going anywhere. You said we're having a spirit quest, so if you really believe that then you either know something you don't want to know, or you just figured something out. Tell me."

She had to say something, and blurted out the first words that came to her mind. "You find people who are lost..."

"I find people who are lost," he confirmed, and waited for her say more. Think it through.

But right now it wasn't about making connections. That one statement unlocked so much more. So much she didn't even really want to think about, let alone put into words. Or what she could even tell him without freaking him out.

That she knew she loved him?

That she knew she wanted him?

That she'd change every part of who she was just for the chance to be with him?

That she wasn't even supposed to be alive, so how could she be with him?

She wasn't supposed to be able to have a family and make more people, more consumers, add to overpopulation. She couldn't settle down, stop going out into the world on her missions to try and make her accidental life a happy accident instead of being the waste her father had always said she would be.

As she felt the firm heat against her back she realized he'd stopped shaking. At least she'd managed that…

She'd never loved any man because she'd always dated men she wasn't especially attracted to—the ones who wouldn't tempt her—and if they were from the places she frequented they understood her lifestyle.

She couldn't even let herself think about the possibility of having her own family. It was wrong.

It confirmed every bad thing her father had said about her. It made him right, and it hurt too much. Daydreaming gave her hope, but it was false.

But somehow Anson had slipped past her defenses and she wanted to change, be someone that he could love. Become someone real.

She had to say something, and she couldn't lie to him.

Instead, she whispered the only thing she could. "I don't want to tell you."

He didn't say anything right away, just held her and nuzzled into her hair until she relaxed against him.

"Is it too hard to say?"

"I don't want you to know."

He stilled. "You don't trust me?"

"You find people who are lost," she repeated, not knowing what else to say, "but you can't find me, Anson. There's nothing to find."

The sigh that preceded his words said as much as his tone. "There damned well is someone to find."

"I don't want to hurt you."

"Is this about what you said the other night?

I forgot about that. You aren't supposed to be alive?"

She went quiet again, trying to sort through it. But the epiphanies that had given her the bum's rush dried up with her gaze fixed on the wall. His heart beat against her back slow and steady while hers hammered so hard her lungs felt they would bruise.

"My father and mother didn't ever want to have children. The world is overpopulated, and people who are trying to change should lead by showing the way. They shouldn't have kids because it helps offset all the people who have lots of kids and all that."

"Why did they?"

"Accident. Mom got pregnant and her conscience wouldn't let her have an abortion. So I'm this black mark on Dad's record. I make him a hypocrite."

"He said that to you?" Anson asked, the incredulity in his voice making her look back at him.

"Honesty is the best policy."

"It's not the best policy when it makes your kids feel...I don't even... I can't even think of what you..."

"I'm fine. I just I don't want to mess up. I need to do better than they did. Not ever get pregnant, or have the strength to do what has to be done if I do. I shouldn't have the opportunity to make more lives to burden the planet with, or burden the planet in any other way either. So I try…"

He flipped her around so she landed on the mattress on her back. He leaned over her, his expression thunderous. "You're not a burden on the planet. If your parents actually said that…"

"Oh, not my mom. She never… Just my dad. He has very strong morals."

Anson might've put his fist through the wall once or twice in his life, but he didn't take out his aggression on people. Ellory's father? He'd make an exception for that man, if he ever met him. "What did you think of when you ran away from me just now?"

"Nothing. Nothing important."

"You tell me right now."

"It's not important. I know why I was supposed to come back here now. That's what is important."

She reached for his face, trying to distract him or soothe him, when she was the one who needed soothing. He pulled her hands away from his face and laid them on her chest, holding them there, holding her beneath him. "You want to know why you're not happy? That's why. No one can be happy under that weight. That lie."

"I was supposed to come back here and find you."

"So I could tell you that what they told you was bull?"

"No. Stop thinking about that. It's not important. What's important is that you're lost too. You find people, but you're lost. Someone else has to find you."

CHAPTER ELEVEN

ANSON KEPT HER pinned beneath him so she couldn't get away—it felt like that kind of a situation, where one wrong move and she'd be gone from him. "You can't be okay with this. It's not an okay situation. You can talk to me."

"You can talk to me too. I've told you so much about myself, but I know very little about you. It has upset you, even though that's silly, so now you want to talk about it. But there's other stuff that upsets you and you never talk about that stuff. I've told you, like…everything about me. If you can't tell me anything, then whatever connection…whatever is going on between us is just a joke."

He didn't want to talk about that stuff. He wanted to talk about this stuff. This *I'm supposed to not be alive* stuff. "If I tell you that stuff, will you talk about this too?"

She looked at him for several long seconds and

then nodded. "If you tell me about the important things, about how you feel about Jude and why it's so personal, and I want to know about your toes...and your mom—were you with her when she died? You tell me that so I don't have to keep trying to badger it out of you, and I will tell you what you want to know. You can't just try to shut me up with kissing or some other method. If you keep bottling things up, eventually you're going to put your fist through another wall."

"That was before we were together."

"It was when you needed someone to talk to and refused to talk to anyone."

Anson sighed and leaned off her, pulling her with him as he rolled onto his back. He liked this position. His arms could go around her and her hair was loose, not lain on or pinned down in any fashion—he could touch it without accidental pulling and he found that soothing.

She did warm him, and he finally noticed the tremor he'd been feeling in his guts had stopped.

Being with her—fed by her, held by her, loved by her—were all comforts, but being challenged by her, being worried about her, was what turned up his internal furnace and finally warmed him.

Telling her the whole truth would make her feel differently about him. Maybe not negative—not telling her was doing that already—but would she take his guilt on? She'd said as much before she'd started inexplicably crying.

"Me not telling you that stuff, how I got stranded on the mountain, it's not that I think you wouldn't understand. I know you would understand, you're probably the most empathic person I've ever met…"

"Then why? It hurts me that you won't tell me. And, more importantly, it hurts you."

"That's not more important." He bit the words out, then stopped and took a breath. He didn't want to yell at her, upset her more. It was his frustration talking. And the fact that he needed to know why she'd started crying, what dark thing she'd thought about herself. She couldn't carry that darkness, it *would* hurt her. Change her. "What makes you think I don't deserve the burden I carry?"

"You're a good man."

He shook his head, and she must have felt it because she lifted her head from his chest and looked up. He kept his eyes on the ceiling, though, not looking her in the eye might be the only way he could get through this.

"You're a freaking hero!"

"I killed my mother."

She went utterly still in his arms, even to the point she stopped breathing. He felt her heartbeat increasing beneath where his palm flattened against her back, keeping her close.

"I don't believe you."

But her behavior said she did believe him. He gave her a little shake and she started breathing again, though more shallowly and faster than normal.

He had to tell her now. And he couldn't look at her when he told her. Rolling again, he managed to get her on her side and lie behind her, where he could once more bury his face in her hair. It was soft, and her scent comforting.

"We were on our yearly ski trip. I was ten."

"Where?"

"Here." He answered the question then continued. "A storm was coming. We, my mom and I, had stayed out until the snow started coming down too hard. She said it was time to go down, go back inside. I said one more run... And before she could grab me I took off down the back side of the pass. If I was going to get in trouble for disobeying, then I was going to get the most mileage out of that punishment I could. That side of the pass, the steep side…no one had let me go down every time I'd tried. They all said it was too advanced for me."

"Did you fall?"

"Of course I did. It *was* too advanced for me. I gave it a good run, made it about two-thirds of the way down before I wiped out on a rock while going too fast. Fell. Slid the rest of the way down the slope. Broke my leg. Thigh. Femur."

"Where your scar is?"

He'd seen her examining it before, she'd touched him everywhere, but he'd been pretty good about distracting her when she'd been working up to the question. "Yes."

He waited for her to absorb that. She thought through things out loud usually, and no way was he going to do this again. Do it once, do it right, put it out of his mind. That meant letting her have questions as they went.

"Did she find you?"

"She caught up to me when I was on my back,

facing downhill, screaming. We were completely alone—if someone had been around they would've heard the screaming."

She started squirming, trying to turn herself around. He didn't want to look her in the eye right now. "Be still." He squeezed then pressed a kiss into the crook of her neck. And then another. And then behind the ear. Sex between them was explosive enough that he could put an end to this conversation for now, continue kissing her, work her up... She'd give up talking but then he'd just have to deal with it again another day, and he wanted answers right now too.

"So what happened? A broken femur can't bear any weight. Was it a straight break? You must have hit... It was here at the pass? I don't remember hearing about this."

"I'm a few years older than you. I was ten. So you were..."

"Six."

"Most six-year-olds don't keep up with the news."

She nodded and sighed. "So it was that big boulder toward the bottom of the insane slope... the one that juts out and is all sharp? I used to think it was a tooth that the mountain had. Mountain tooth."

"That's the one," he confirmed. "Tooth works. And, yes, I couldn't put any weight on it. She wasn't a large woman, so the best we could do was me pushing with one leg while she pulled me. The storm was really picking up, the sky got so dark it could've been night, but she managed to find a tight overhang, a ledge close to the ground. She crawled in then dragged me in after her."

Her fingers twined with his, showing the support he'd known she'd show him. It was easier to accept the support from her hands than to see it in her eyes.

"The first night was the worst. So cold. We couldn't even really huddle together for warmth because of how shallow the space was. My leg hurt so bad. She fished a toy from my backpack and used it like a puppet, told me stories…

"We thought the storm would break in the morning. I was losing consciousness in spells that day, so it was a better day for me. I try not to think about what it was like for her."

She managed to roll over when his arms relaxed, taking advantage of that small window before he could stop her. Her hand pulled free of his and she used it to brush his hair back from his face, her palm soft, and in that moment he knew she loved him. Which meant he had to tell her what he'd caused so she could know what she was getting into. If he told her he loved her before telling that, it'd color and corrupt her thoughts.

"From there, the story is what I've managed to cobble together from what other people have told me and what I remember. When the storm stopped on the third day I was completely out. I don't remember that night or morning at all. I imagine she tried to wake me. I didn't actually wake up until several days later in the hospital, which was a couple of days after my final surgery. There was one to repair my thigh, the pins needed to set the bone and remove some tissue that had died. And the second one was to remove toes that had succumbed to frostbite. Only one on the healthy leg, but the broken one got it worse. Probably because of restricted blood flow to the area."

"I didn't put that together. I saw the scars…"

"I know." Part of being loved by Ellory meant she touched him everywhere. She hadn't simply stroked her fingers over that scar, she'd kissed it on multiple occasions. She just hadn't known it was all connected.

"How did they find you?"

"She'd tucked her outer jacket over my legs to try and keep them warm…"

"Femur breaks are terrible…"

"Yes. And lots of blood pooled. She was a doctor too, an ER doctor, so she would've known how dire my situation was becoming. After doing what she could to keep me warm, she crawled out and tried to make it up and over the mountain."

"Did they find her?"

"Yes. She'd frozen before she reached the top. Being three days without food and water…she just wasn't strong enough to make it. They followed her trail back to find me."

She combed his hair again and pulled him down until his head was on her chest and she could continue the petting. He should argue with her about it. He didn't deserve her comfort. If he had to relive it while finding Jude…who had left his friends to try and get help, just like his mother had done…he deserved to feel miserable.

"What you're feeling now? Everyone goes through it. It's the bottom."

"Rock bottom?"

"When you're on a quest, you have to purge all the bad stuff before you can start to heal."

Healing. She was so sweet. He wouldn't heal, and he didn't want to. He deserved whatever punishment his mind, or the universe, as she liked to say, deigned to dish out. There could never be redemption for what he'd done. There just was no way to make up for it. His mother was gone. She'd always be gone. His father had lost the woman he loved, and it was *his* fault.

It was his weakness that kept him from pulling away from her. Just another sin, a mark of his cowardice. The search was pulling him back into the void he'd suffered in his darkest days during recovery, and Ellory was his lifeline. If she was pulling away from him, he had to keep her with him. At least until he found Jude and could afford the time it would take to lose his damned mind properly.

"What are you thinking?"

"That I need this," Anson muttered. He

shouldn't, but if she knew…maybe she'd stick with him a little longer.

"This? Do you mean to feel bad?"

"No. I mean this." He slid his hand over her skin until it settled over her breast, and the soft firmness that instantly changed, the nipple growing hard to poke the hollow of his palm.

Before she could ask anything else, he pulled her under him, slid an arm under her neck and kissed her. He could lose himself in her—his only way to keep from thinking. Burying himself in her was his only form of meditation, her soft body, her tender heart, and the brief, blessed oblivions she could give him.

"You owe me words, Ellory Star."

"I know," she whispered, still touching his face. "Can we save it for tomorrow? I'd really like it if you would just kiss me right now."

Day fourteen of searching since the storm had passed.

Nothing had been the same since that night—except in every physical way.

Another long hot shower, though she didn't join him wasting the water any more. Their showers got longer and longer—more and more waste-ful—when she was with him. And she wanted to ignore that little voice that insisted she was mak-ing herself into whatever she needed to be to fit into his lifestyle. But she didn't really know what his lifestyle was—in her mind it was the worst it could be for her. Becoming the antithesis of all the things she'd believed in her whole life…even if it would make life easier and keep her from being this obsessive crazy person, it felt like exchang-ing one set of bad habits for another.

At least if she listened to that annoying little voice right now, she could feel confident that she wouldn't be manufacturing more guilt for herself later when she finally did figure out what she was supposed to do with herself, how she was sup-posed to find a way out from beneath the crush-ing guilt, and find contentment. It was all hard enough without having to think about the things she'd been conditioned to do. Habits, even while tiring and tiresome, were easier than the uncer-tainty.

Another hot and hearty meal to cut the chill and fortify him. He ate too fast, so did she—it was simply nutrition, tasteless no matter how she tried to make it good, and they both needed to get back to that mattress, their only comfort.

She'd tried to explain to him that her father's distance and disapproval had driven her to live the best life she could, and that while she could see why it upset him, she thought she'd turned it into something positive. Or she'd always thought that until now. She'd tried to explain it until they both were so frustrated with one another they stopped talking altogether.

She didn't know what to say or how to help him. She wanted to help, and she'd made early attempts to try and tell him he couldn't live his life with that kind of blackness in his heart without it consuming him. He'd nodded, repeated it back to her, and disregarded her advice.

As soon as they found Jude, Ellory was going to break it off. It would be an acceptable time then. She wouldn't be abandoning him when he needed the support she absolutely knew he did need. But afterwards…breaking up was just what had to happen.

It already hurt so bad to be with him that she was trying to soothe herself when they went to bed as much as she was trying to soothe him.

Those all-too-brief moments of bliss when they were together carried her through the next day. Well, almost through. Like a drug, the more she had of him, the quicker the effect wore off until she needed more. She'd had friends who had gone down dark paths—had watched them spiral down, and when lucky, their recovery.

It was the only mental comparison she could make. Withdrawal. How bad would it be to recover from his touch? Would she have any chance of staying on the wagon if she stayed in town where she had access to her drug of choice?

She should start looking now for a new mission. Some exotic new location, people she could actually help and feel good about herself again. Somewhere she didn't have to work so hard to figure out how to live... If she were in some remote village away from all modern conveniences—where they struggled to provide running water— she'd live simply and have no way to be a planetary burden.

They were just finishing dinner when someone knocked at the door.

Mira?

"Graves?" A low man's voice called.

"It's Frank." Anson stood up and answered the door. "Are we going back out?"

Frank Powell was his supervisor, and he had taken over managing the search operation once roads up to the lodge had been cleared enough to get additional search teams in.

Wishful thinking. Ellory saw it on his face the moment she joined them. They weren't going back out.

Frank stepped inside and closed the door. "No, not tonight," he answered first, and then dipped his head to her. "Evenin', Ellory." They'd met many times in the past two weeks as she'd made it part of her job description to bring food to the base of operations they'd set up in one of the conference rooms.

Her visits had never been wholly selfless. With all the tooling they did about the mountains on the snowmobiles, she was in a constant state of anxiety that a slide would happen and bury them all. Showing up with food or drinks gave her an excuse to be there and hear any information, and sometimes to just hear Anson's voice come through on the radio and know that he was okay. Or as okay as he could be.

She was about to offer food when the older gentleman turned to Anson. "I wanted to come tell you in person—word's officially come down that the search for Wyndham is being reclassified as a recovery mission."

They'd been waiting for this moment, but her heart still sank. She may have only been a few feet away from Anson but hurried over to him and slipped her hand into his.

"There's still a chance," he said, for once not accepting her comforting touch. His hand pulled free and he scrubbed it over his face, trying to wipe off the lie he'd just uttered. They all knew better. Jude could've never survived two weeks in the cold without food or water. He couldn't have survived one week, and probably not even a few days. He was gone, and had been for probably the whole time they'd been searching.

Frank knew his words for what they were—grief. Grief for a man he had never met. Grief for a man he felt like he'd let down. Grief for himself... His normally booming voice was gentle, gentler than Ellory would've ever thought he could make it. "You know that's not true, son."

Anson stepped away from both of them, and

Max, sensing the discord in the air, stood up where he was in front of the fire and went straight to Anson's side, ducking his nose and pushing forward until Anson's hand cupped his head.

Anson took the request and petted his trusty companion. Which was good. At least he was touching and taking comfort from someone who loved him.

"Most of the outside teams are leaving and we're reworking our plan," Frank continued. "You and Max should be on duty where you can help the living. I want you to take a couple of days to rest and then report for regular duty."

Anson folded his arms and shook his head. "No. We need to see this through, Max and I. We're not off the search team." The dog moved in front of Anson and sat, a silent and calm sentinel doing what sentinels did. Protective instinct. Ellory couldn't blame him. Hers were running on high too. She just couldn't pull off the calm sentinel routine like Max did. She'd have said something if she knew what to say.

Was she supposed to back him up? The search was killing him, but not searching? She had no idea how that would affect him.

* * *

The next day, while Anson was disobeying orders, Ellory did what any sensible kind of almost-girlfriend would do when confronted with a man in pain: she dug around for information about him on the internet. Found his father's name and that he was a doctor still practicing in San Francisco. Found his mother in an article talking about the rescue, and a memoriam set up to remember her by her old hospital.

None of it was particularly insightful, though she did find one gem: an old photo attached to the rescue article showing exactly where Anson had been found, the place they'd hidden and where his mother's trail had led the rescuers back to. And she found something else: a young Frank to one side, caught in mid-gesture as he'd crouched and pointed into the dark space.

God bless Frank and whoever had taken the picture. They might as well have left a road map for her.

CHAPTER TWELVE

SINCE HER DISCOVERIES had come early in the morning, by noon Ellory had rented a snowmobile and set off on one of the lesser-used trails of Silver Pass. Thanks to the article and the photo she'd found, she was pretty sure she knew right where Anson and his mother had weathered the storm. Maybe there was some trace of the time they'd spent there. His toy? Marks on the stone… something. Even just a simple understanding of what it was like to be in there would be a start.

Even Ellory knew she was grasping at straws, but aside from grilling Frank—which would no doubt be the next step if she didn't find anything in the overhang—it was the only idea she had that might help her help *him*.

The slope Anson had crashed on in his childhood wasn't marked for guests to find easily these days, and she really didn't know if that had always been the case or if it was something that

Mr. Dupris had done after the accident. It was maintained and usable—if you knew what you were doing and how to get there. But all signs led to other slopes.

She knew she'd found it when she started seeing the warning signs.

Stopping the snowmobile at the top of the slope, Ellory surveyed the way down, trying to decide whether there was a safe route to the bottom or not.

With the machine idling in low gear, she heard some short staccato sound echoing through the pass.

She killed the engine and immediately realized what it was: frantic barking. Max…it was Max. But the echo made it impossible to follow.

If Max was barking like that, then something was really wrong. Anson should be calming him down.

Her heart skipped. If Anson wasn't calming him down…

This rugged part of the pass was the most remote, the most dangerous… Her instinct told her that down the crazy run was the direction to go.

The cold air suddenly felt suffocating. Adjusting the face mask and goggles, she started the machine again and took a chance with the machine in the trees. If she went slowly, she could make it down that way. And it couldn't get out of control and end up rolling too far if there were trees in the way. She'd just crash into one, and hopefully not be going that fast when it happened.

Now wasn't the time to stop trusting her gut.

As carefully as she could with any speed, Ellory wove between the trees in a wide zigzag down the slope. The further down she went, the louder the barking got.

About halfway down she realized the barking was getting quieter again.

She'd passed them.

She turned the beast hard toward the cleared slope and worked her way to the tree line.

About a hundred yards up the slope she saw a snowdrift and the black dog in stark relief against it. He was barking at the snow between periods of frantic digging.

Avalanche dog.

She scrambled off the machine and up the slope as hard and fast as she could. *"Anson!"*

When Max saw her, he barked more frantically

and ran to meet her, grabbing her sleeve and half dragging her toward the snow she clawed her way up and over.

If he was in there…as long as the barking had been going on… God, she knew someone died in avalanches every couple years. They'd already lost one in a slip this season.

Rounding the drift to where Max dragged her, she saw a hole dug into the bank and Anson's head. Max had got to his head.

"Anson!" She strangled on his name, a barely controlled sob almost choking her.

His head turned and he looked at her. Alive. Alive and awake. No neck injury…he could move his neck.

"We'll get you out." She began pushing the snow off the mound holding him down. Max joined in again, digging beside her.

"It wasn't a real slide…there was a weird cornice…"

She didn't have time to look around and figure out what the hell he was talking about. The only thing she could think of was getting through the heavy wet volume of snow and pulling him free.

"How long?"

"I don't know." He sounded tired. She knew he was tired.

Her goggles fogged from the tears streaming from her eyes, so she tore them off and used the cup like a shovel. She should have had a shovel…

"Tell me what you're feeling."

"The snow is heavy," he said, but as she dug through several feet and lessened the load on his chest, he began to breathe more easily.

When his hands were free, he held them up to her. "Pull."

Taking both his hands, she leaned back as hard as she could, putting all her weight into the pull. Max pulled too, grabbing Anson's hood and giving quick powerful tugs that made her worry about his spine.

He slid free enough to use his legs, and soon he was out with her and Ellory grabbed for his hands, tearing through the buckles to get his gloves off and inspect his fingers. Red. Still red.

She fell at his feet, and shoved his still wobbly body back into the snow so she could rip one of his boots off. The foot with the most toes had red toes. She checked the other. Two red toes, red feet.

"I'm okay," he said, but he still didn't sound

okay. She didn't believe him, not one bit. But she couldn't leave him with his boots off, so she shook the sock to make sure no snow had gotten on it, and helped get his boots back on before she even tried to look him in the eye.

"We're going to the hospital." She looked up now, at the cornice that had fallen on him. "Is your snowmobile under there?"

He nodded. The fact that he wasn't arguing with her about going to the hospital actually did worry her.

"Max will just have to walk with us. I have one, down the slope a way. We'll go slowly."

"How did you know to come?"

"I heard Max."

"You were out already?"

"I was…looking. For something." She wasn't going to tell him precisely what she'd been looking for, and she wasn't going to ask why Anson had gone looking for Jude on this slope. She had the idea that they were headed in the same direction, but neither of them was emotionally ready to talk about it yet.

He moved stiffly and slowly, but when she took his arm again to get it over her shoulder, she realized he was shaking again. Really shaking. The kind of intense shivering the body did to warm itself. Hypothermia…and more than a mild case.

"It's not far." She held him as best she could and they wove a sliding path for the machine, Max keeping pace with them.

When she got him on the machine, she dug into the back and pulled out an insulated jug of hot tea. "It's ginseng and honey for energy." She didn't drink the preservative-laden cocoa, and was trying to get herself back to the habits that had had to be abandoned when things had gotten hairy during the blizzard. "It will warm you some."

Anson took the tea and drank. First a few sips, then more deeply.

When it was half-gone he handed it back. She capped it back up and stowed it in the back compartment.

Max looked around for his cage…but since it was on the buried ATV she said, "Come, Max." Hoping he'd follow them.

"Track," Anson said, wrapping his arms around her middle. The tea helped a little. He wasn't shaking so hard now that she thought he would lose his seat on the machine.

Even so, as a precaution she took a moment and cross-buckled the straps on his gloves, securing them together with his arms around her waist, in case Anson passed out while they rode. The last thing he needed was to fall off and add head trauma to his hypothermia…

Max barked once, she repeated the command, "Track, Max. Track." And then fired her rental to life and started back the long way she'd come.

Too many hurdles had been thrown at her in the past month, she couldn't keep up or even keep track of what she was supposed to be worrying about from moment to moment. Jude. Anson's emotional state. Her carbon footprint. Whether the dog would keep up with them. And now whether Anson had frostbite. Again. Never mind how she was going to cope when she had to go…

She and the universe were going to have to have a long talk after this was over.

Anson had never actually been covered by snow before, not to that extent. Had the situation been any different, had it not been for Max, had Ellory not been mysteriously out on the mountain on a machine she hated…

He'd have to ask her about that later.

Right now, sitting in the examination room at his emergency department, waiting for X-ray results to be read, he was glad he'd banished her to the waiting room.

If he had, in fact, broken ribs, as he suspected he had, then she couldn't know. She'd try to use it to keep him off the mountain, and that couldn't happen.

Technically, the doctor checking him out—a colleague he worked with during his six months of the year when he wasn't on winter duty—was supposed to report his injury to Frank, who would then suspend him from duty. But Anson had gotten hurt while on his own time, since he'd been ordered off the search and had been actively disobeying. And he could ride around the mountains on his snowmobile without much physical exertion. When he found Jude, he'd just have to call for someone else to recover the body.

He owed it to Chelsea and the rest of the group to find the man. He'd looked her in the eye and told her he'd bring Jude home. He'd bring the man home. And on the way out, when this exam was over, he'd stop by Chelsea's room to let her know he wasn't giving up.

Twenty minutes later, having been given a lecture he could've done without, Anson had been zipped back into his suit and in a wheelchair, being wheeled back out to the waiting area. Hospital policy, blah-blah-blah. He could walk, but considering he was getting by without being officially reported to superiors he decided not to push his luck.

Ellory stood as soon as he was wheeled out and came over to take over the pushing. "Are you ready to go?"

"I want to see Chelsea first. But I have to ride there in this chair...stay in it until I have officially left the hospital after being seen."

She wheeled him through the sliding doors toward the elevators. "I know where it is."

"How do you know where it is?"

"I checked while you were being treated. I had a couple of hours to do it." She waited until they were alone in the elevator to ask him more questions. "What did they say is wrong?"

"They said I'm all right. It wasn't the best thing

in the world to have happen, and I'm very sore, but it's not going to kill me. They said to make sure and force a cough once an hour, which is what I expected."

"Why?"

"Because when your ribs are hurt, you don't want to breathe deeply. That can cause some people to get pneumonia. But if you keep coughing regularly, it keeps your lungs clear."

The elevator dinged and she pushed him out and to the left, not mentioning to him that she'd actually gone to check in on Chelsea once while waiting for him and going nuts with worry about him. Mira was watching Max, so Ellory hadn't even had her furry support system with her to distract her for her wait. Rescue dogs, while service animals, aren't in the same class as personal service dogs—like seeing-eye dogs—who can go anywhere.

She didn't even feel bad about not telling him that she'd gone to see Chelsea. He wasn't telling her everything, and he'd not let her go into the examination room with him. Because this wasn't a relationship. This wasn't a relationship. This wasn't a relationship.

Maybe repeating the words again and again would make them finally sink in. She was not his girlfriend. He didn't love her, he couldn't love her. It was never going to happen. This was not a relationship.

As she pushed him into Chelsea's room the woman sat up in her bed, eyes wide and round as she looked at him.

"You look like hell," she informed him. "Looks like this search is wearing everyone to the bone. Maybe you should let someone else do the searching for a while."

He shook his head then commandeered the wheels of his chair to wheel right up to Chelsea's bed, where he could reach over and take his patient's hand. "I'm all right. Max the wonder dog and Ellory got me out of my little accident."

"What happened?"

"On the back side of the pass there's a place about midway down the slope, a geographical oddity where there's flat ground beneath a short, slanted overhang…short in terms of mountains. I stopped the snowmobile there because it was flat and Max needed to water some trees… It was a dumb place to stop. The mantel slid and dumped snow on me, knocking me down but not sweeping me away. It wasn't enough for that. Not even a proper avalanche, more like all the five feet thick blanket of snow off a big slanted roof dropping on you unexpectedly."

"You were lucky," Chelsea said, her expression soft. Ellory wished she could see inside Anson's head and read the emotions there as easily as she could read Chelsea's. She felt guilty that he was still out there.

Anson shook his head. "Max dug the snow out before I suffocated and then barked loud enough for Ellory to find us."

Ellory didn't know what to do or say. He wouldn't want her comfort here in front of people, and she didn't really know what to say or do for him right now to help.

Chelsea settled her gaze on Anson, still in his chair. "When the storm passed your crew were the only ones who could search for Jude, but they came to visit the other day, and told me how there was no way he could have survived in the snow this long. That it was turning into a recovery mission."

Something else Ellory didn't know was how

Chelsea managed to speak so steadily. Now that Ellory knew what it meant to love a man, and remembering the panic she'd felt when she'd realized Anson was under the snow…

"It doesn't matter if you find him today or in two weeks now. It's not worth dying over. They said I'll be here for a few more weeks at least, maybe even until spring arrives and the snow melts… If there's no chance that he's alive…" Chelsea's throat finally closed, stopping her words.

There was absolutely nothing she could do or say to help either of them. She opened her mouth to say something, though she had no idea what would help, when a knock behind her had her turning and stepping away from the door.

Sheriff, a deputy, and Frank.

Her stomach bottomed out. The presence of three officials together…

They must have found him.

"Jude Wyndham has been found."

Anson heard the voice, heard the words, and carefully turned the wheelchair he'd been confined to so he could face the doorway and whoever had walked into Chelsea's hospital room.

Sheriff Leonard. Deputy Gates. Frank.

"Where was he?" Anson asked, even though he knew that they'd come to tell Chelsea. One look at her face confirmed for Anson that she wasn't able to ask the questions she'd later need the answers to.

"Montana."

Montana. He searched his mind for the name of different peaks and valleys in the area, and came up with nothing. "Where is that? I don't think I'm familiar…"

He noticed Frank looking at him. Frank, his boss, who didn't know he'd been hurt today. Not like it mattered now that Jude had been found.

Frank kept the censure Anson knew he was due out of his voice and his words at least. "The state."

"Montana," Anson repeated, and then again, this time in unison with Chelsea and Ellory, "Montana?"

"How did he get so far away?" Ellory asked.

He couldn't have walked that far during the storm or after without someone noticing. Only an idiot wouldn't walk west or east to get out of the mountains if he was lost. The area was developed well enough that he'd have stumbled over a road and gotten help before he made it all the freaking way to Montana.

"I don't understand. How did he get to Montana?" Chelsea repeated the sentiment.

"By car. He and a woman were picked up in a bank, trying to cash a stolen check they'd tried and failed to cash in Canada," Sheriff Leonard said.

"A woman?" Chelsea asked, her voice rising in pitch.

"Maybe we should speak about this further in private," the sheriff said gently to Chelsea, but Anson didn't need further explanation. He got it.

A look at Ellory confirmed that she was still as confused as Chelsea was.

"Elle?" He said her name softly, getting her attention. "Let's leave them to speak with Chelsea." He tilted his head toward the wheelchair handles, silently asking her to push him out of the room.

She stepped behind him, and after giving Chelsea's hand a supportive squeeze wheeled Anson out of the room. Once out of earshot of those still inside the room she stopped and crouched beside him to whisper, "What were they trying to say to her?"

"That he was never lost in the pass." He said the words gently. "The stolen check he and some woman were trying to cash? They were probably Chelsea's."

"He planned it? He abandoned them out there in the cold and...stole from them and left?" Her voice rose, much as Chelsea's had done. Not only was she shocked that someone would do that, she was angry. Anson could recognize the emotion, even if right now he was surprised to find he didn't share it. He didn't actually feel anything.

"Looks like it. Let's get out of here." He nodded in the way they'd come.

"They could've died..." She continued to speak quietly as she pushed him out of the hospital and on to Mira's car, which she'd borrowed to bring him to the hospital, listing the man's offenses as they occurred to her.

She left him sitting at the patient pick-up and drop-off area to get the car, and Anson took his chance to cough and clear his lungs. It hurt. And she'd insist on staying with him tonight to take care of him if she knew what was going on with him.

* * *

A half an hour later, following Anson's directions, she pulled off the highway onto a one-lane road that had recently been plowed. "What do I do if we meet someone?"

"We won't meet anyone. My house is the only one out here," Anson mumbled, "but I have a service to come plow the lane for the big snows."

The road wound through trees on either side, thick enough that Ellory wasn't sure whether or not there was a ledge anywhere in sight. She drove slowly, afraid of sliding into a ravine in the dark.

It didn't take long to break through the trees to a blanket of barely disturbed whiteness. The lane, which she now realized was more of a long driveway, sloped down and back up, following a gently undulating terrain toward a very small house.

Really small.

"Anson, is part of your house underground?"

"No. It's a micro-house. I thought you'd be familiar with them."

"Of course I am. I guess I just thought…with the size of your dog…" Teeny-tiny environmentally friendly house? Who was this guy?"

"Does Max even fit in there?"

It had been a really tough day, but this discovery was a bright spot.

"He stays mostly in the living room. Sometimes I think it's a glorified doghouse, like when it rains and he gets that wet-dog smell. The bedroom is in the loft, which you get to by ladder. That took some getting used to for him. We lived in an apartment when I first got him, he got used to sleeping with me…and then suddenly he couldn't even get near me when I slept. I think that's why he's been so possessive about sleeping with us…"

He didn't go on at length about much, but the man did love his dog.

He opened his door and climbed out, so she did the same, intent on seeing him safely inside and getting a gander at the interior.

On the tiny porch stoop he fished his keys out of his pocket and let himself in, disabled the alarm, and then looked back at her. "I saw the weather while we were at the hospital. You should probably head back to the lodge now. It's going to get bad again in a little while."

Before she'd even gotten her toe over the threshold he'd slammed down the unwelcome mat? "You aren't coming with me?"

"I really just want to sleep. In my bed."

They may have found Jude, he may not have been on the mountain in need of rescue and all that, but there was an unpleasant sort of hanging feeling left over. At least if they had found him dead, there would've been resolution, a completed task, a way of honoring his promise and all that.

This way? It was just over. It was just done, and as calm as he acted he couldn't be okay with the way things were.

"Are you feeling like punching the wall?"

"No," he said softly.

"What about Max?" And what about her? Was this the end? Now that there was no finding that monster on the mountain, it was just a switch he could flip and be done with her?

He didn't answer as immediately. "He could stay with you tonight if you don't mind, and I'll pick him up in the morning."

Stay with her. Somewhere he wasn't.

"I could stay." She tried again, and barely cared that she sounded pathetic, even to her own ears. "Mira could watch Max. I know she wouldn't mind."

His eyes were tired, his shoulders not nearly

as broad and weight-bearing as they usually appeared. Much too quiet.

"You want me to go." The words were out of her mouth before she actually thought about saying them. "I don't feel good about it. About leaving you here without anyone, even Max."

"It's not that I want you gone, but I'm tired. The idea of crawling into bed and sleeping a day or twelve appeals."

He'd slept with her every night for more than two weeks, but now that Jude had been found... alive...

"Are we supposed to be glad he's alive?" she asked finally. "Because I don't think I am. I've never wished anyone dead or anything, but before, when we were looking for a guy who'd tried to be a hero and save his loved ones, I so wanted him to be found alive. Now I just want to go to Montana and drown him in his own jail toilet."

Anson nodded, though his expression remained sedate. Too sedate. It was worse than when she'd been trying to get him to talk about how Jude being lost affected him. At least then he'd had some kind of emotional expression. He'd put his fist through the freaking wall, so she had at least known he'd been upset, even if he'd denied it. Now, though, now he just seemed numb. And numb scared her.

Whatever he was feeling had to have been worse than what she was feeling. He'd been the one out there searching, reliving losing his mother, overwhelmed by guilt… But he wasn't going to share it with her.

Everything he said, including the stuff only said by his body, let her know he wanted space. Who was she to deny him?

Ellory covered the short space that separated them and leaned up to kiss him.

He tangled his hand in her hair and kept her close, even if he didn't hold her like she wanted… his kiss warm and full of feeling even if she hadn't been able to see it when she'd looked at him, or heard it in his voice.

Maybe she was just reading too much into things. He could just really need some sleep. Maybe tomorrow he'd feel like talking.

CHAPTER THIRTEEN

ANSON WASN'T SITTING about in his underwear, refusing to shower, drinking too much beer, and punching his walls full of holes.

And that was the best thing he could say about his response to the news about Jude.

Jude.

Judas. Was that the man's name? He was going to have to look it up. At some point.

Max, on the other hand? Pretty much doing half of that list. It was next to impossible to get him off his fireside doggy bed. He didn't eat, not even his beloved jerky treats. There had been exactly zero hours of play since their return home. And he got really disgruntled when Anson forced him to go outside.

It looked like mourning to Anson, and probably because his new person was gone. Ellory. He hadn't seen Ellory in several days, and Max hadn't seen her either.

With a sigh Anson peeled himself off the couch and retrieved the phone. He'd call her, let the dog talk to her or hear her voice, and maybe that would help.

She answered just as the call was about to shuffle off somewhere else—the front desk? Voicemail? Anson had no clue where unanswered calls went at the lodge.

When he heard her voice come down the line his chest squeezed, which set off a coughing fit before he'd managed to say a word.

"Anson?"

He cleared his throat. "Ellory. Sorry."

On hearing her name, Max got up from the bed and nearly knocked Anson over. "Max wants to talk to you on the phone."

"Max wants to talk to me." He heard it in her voice—she might as well have called him the bastard they both knew him to be.

The massive Newfoundland standing on his hind legs and putting weight on Anson's upper body got him moving toward the point. "If you wouldn't mind. He's been really depressed. Won't eat or anything." He pushed the dog off him and walked to the couch. At least there Max could crawl up on the seat beside him and maybe not break his cracked ribs the rest of the way.

He punched the speaker button and laid the phone on the coffee table. "You're on speaker."

"Hi, Maxie-Max," Ellory crooned, and the dog's tail went wagging with enough force Anson thought his legs might bruise. The big furry head tilted in that confused and interested way he had and he looked up at the loft, then behind him, smelling the air. But he couldn't find Ellory.

"Want a jerky, Max? Tell your big dumb jerky-face who loves you very much. I'm sure he'll give you a jerky. Jerky? Jerky?"

Every time she said "jerky," the dog got more and more excited while she left Anson abundantly clear on exactly what kind of jerky she was talking about: not the kind his dog lived for.

"Just a second," Anson said. "Keep talking, I'll get the stuff."

He stood and walked into the kitchen, leaving Ellory to psych up his dog into eating.

When he came back, she was saying "jerky" so fast and so frequently that the word had stopped sounding like a word. But Max still took the piece when Anson offered it to him.

"He's eating," he yelled, to get over the sound of her silly jerky song. Then he picked up the phone and switched off the speaker. "Thank you."

Asking how she was would be the right thing to do, she'd been upset about Judas too. But asking her that would certainly open the door for her to ask him, and he just had no answers to give her on that score.

Ellory made her way back through her bedroom obstacle course to sit on the bed. After the storm the lodge had started filling up again. She could be working right now if she wanted to. Guests had returned to the lodge and the slopes as soon as the slopes had been prepared and the power had come back on.

By now someone would've overworked an ill-used muscle or joint. Injured themselves…something. But she just didn't have the desire. She was exhausted from worrying, trying not to worry, trying to pretend she didn't care, etcetera—so she didn't worry Mira or work herself up into such a state about Anson that she made herself crazy.

"I'm just a symptom," she said into the phone, after silence had reigned for entirely too long.

Anson spoke with caution, because this whole business was awkward. "A symptom of what?"

"He doesn't miss me so much as he has a big chapter of his life unfinished."

"Finding Jude?"

Ellory nodded, then actually spoke out loud because this wasn't video conferencing... "He spent weeks of his life looking for someone who never got found. He needs closure." And she did too.

And just like that she knew what she had to do. She'd never gotten to her destination that day. Only the universe knew whether or not she'd find anything of his time in the tiny cave. Maybe getting to find someone where he'd lost his mother would help him move on too.

"There isn't going to be any closure about that. Though I think they are extraditing him to the area, so maybe we could go and find him at the jail."

"He needs to find someone. Anyone will do. I'm going out on the mountain in my old crappy snow suit that doesn't keep very warm compared to what my beautiful new suit does."

"Elle..."

She ignored the warning in his voice. "I'm

going back to where you got trapped. Take Max there and come and find me. When he finds me, he'll feel better."

And maybe he would too.

Before he could say anything, she hung up, dropped her phone, and crawled under her bed to retrieve the snow suit from hell.

On the plus side, if she froze to death out there, when they found her, everyone would get a good laugh out of how ridiculous she looked.

If it weren't for the fact that he was generally against killing people...

Anson's snowmobile was still buried on the slope where he was going to find Ellory, which meant he had to go slowly enough on the rented thing for Max to keep up.

Unlike the weather that had plagued them for the past several weeks, the day was bright, sunny and warm enough that the snow held high in the trees was dripping and dropping off, forcing him to take the long way around to where he knew to begin the search.

When they got near the area where Max and Ellory had pulled him from the snow, Max took off and left him speeding in something other than the safest manner in order to keep up with him.

On the other side of the big mound of snow sat another empty snowmobile.

Max sniffed it and then ran back to Anson, to and from until he'd gotten the machine throttled down and had climbed off. Footprints led down the mountain, the snow being still deep enough in this area that she'd left deep leg prints in the snow.

And if she was in the old-fashioned snowsuit, it would not be water-resistant, so she'd be cold. Anywhere her body touched snow would be wet, and that wetness would sink in toward her body fast.

"Dammit, Ellory," he muttered to himself, and led Max to her abandoned snowmobile, tapping the seat twice and giving the command "Find."

Max didn't even smell the seat—it wasn't like he couldn't follow the tracks she'd left. He tore off down the mountain after her, barking and so excited that Anson felt bad for having kept the big guy away from her.

It had taken Ellory an hour of digging in order to make an opening in the snow big enough to crawl through into Anson's tiny cave. She got about halfway in before her suit caught on a jagged piece of rock hanging down. Ellory felt it rip as she backed up, deepened the hole with a couple more shovels of snow, and finally made it inside.

He hadn't been kidding when he'd said it had been a tight fit.

With how long it had taken her to get to the area and make it inside, she half expected that he'd get there just before her feet disappeared inside and drag her out.

She looked toward the light. Feet inside.

Very dark.

Rolling to her side, she got a small flashlight out of her pocket and flicked it on to shine around the creepy interior.

Now that she was there, she felt the strangest feeling of peace—like she was right where she was supposed to be, when she was supposed to be there. Though she really had no idea why, aside from providing Anson the closure he and Max both needed.

Closure. So final. She shivered.

With effort, she shifted to a slightly taller area of the overhang and managed to roll over. That left the area she'd dug out open for Max or Anson, or anyone else who decided to come crawling inside.

If she had been Anson's mother, when they'd crawled in here she'd have put her son on that side of the cave. It was smaller, would've kept him from moving around too much with his broken femur.

She shone the light around, looking for anything he might've left behind…some evidence of having been there…but she didn't see his toy or his backpack. She didn't even see any marks on the rocks where he might've passed the time.

But she did see a dark little cubbyhole opening in the rocks.

And something shiny sparkled in the dirt beneath the hole.

Rolling back to her cold belly, she crawled over to that side again and stuck her mittened hand into the cubbyhole.

It went deep, all the way to her elbow before her hand touched bottom. Weird.

She patted around, trying to decide if that was maybe a place that air had come in and had maybe made Anson colder during his wait.

There was no outlet she could feel, and with the snow blanketing everything outside no air came through either.

When she began working her arm back out of the hole, something bumped into her knuckle and she cried in alarm and jerked her hand out. A few seconds of listening confirmed it—no sound of movement came from the dark and suddenly dangerous-seeming cubbyhole.

What had it felt like? Animal? No… If it had been an animal, it would've bitten her. She looked at her mitten. Intact. No pain in the hand in it.

Dead animal? Felt way too solid for that. When she didn't hear any movement, she took a deep breath and shoved her hand back inside. This time her hand curled over the object immediately and she extracted her arm from the hole.

She fished a toy from my backpack and used it like a puppet…told me stories.

Ellory looked at the plastic army man in his camouflage fatigues and black flat-top haircut and really wanted to cry this time.

He had peeling paint on his legs and back, but his molded plastic face was pristine.

The sound of barking cut through the air, letting her know Max was on his way to find and save her. She stuffed the doll into her suit, and then looked around. Where had that shiny thing gone…?

She flashed the light around in the area she'd seen it, didn't find it, and then started roughing up the dirt in the area as well. Silver Pass wasn't just called that because of the silvery white snow that fell in great quantities. And she'd discovered a tiny silver nugget once…

By the time her flashlight caught the reflection again, she'd almost worked up enough dirt into the air to send a dust bunny into asthmatic convulsions.

A delicate silver chain. She lifted it out of the dirt and her breath caught as the chain grew taut and a good-sized oval pendant hopped free from the earth.

Correction: oval locket.

Giving it a quick wipe, she pulled one mitten off and found the seam with her thumbnail, popping the catch.

The picture inside had been through however many seasons of snow and ice. The colors had faded. Her throat burned.

She knew the eyes looking out from the picture.

* * *

Anson caught up just in time to see Max's fluffy tail disappear under the overhang of rocks where he'd known Ellory would be.

"You found me!" he heard her say, her voice animated. "Good boy!" And then, a moment later, "Anson?"

"What?" He folded his arms, not in the mood for this.

"Can you call him back out? It's hard to crawl around in here."

He shook his head, feeling an epic eye-roll coming on. "Come, Max. Out!"

Many long seconds passed before his oversized dog crawled back out, wagging his tail so hard he could have cleared land with it. Completely happy.

"You too. Come, Ellory. Out!"

He saw padded black boots first. The dog might've been able to squirm around and crawl out head first, but Ellory didn't have the room in there to do it.

The further out she got, the less angry he became. Her snowsuit, if it could be called that, looked like a quilt. An actual quilt...but canvas, and possibly made from army surplus duffel bags, and maybe even circus tents? And the best part: some kind of purple and yellow checkered canvas.

She came up butt first, and when she turned around it was all Anson could do not to laugh. On her head? A knitted cap in of many colors— as if if it had been made using a little bit of every yarn in the store, and topped with a puffy ball. He had to remind himself he was mad at her for going in there.

"I can see why you don't often wear that snow-suit." He laughed a little, the sound would not be contained. "Must be hard to bear the envy of all around you when the skiers get a look at that magnificent creation."

She ignored him, though her cheeks looked quite pink by this point beneath the smears of dirt she'd undoubtedly picked up in the tight lit-tle cave.

Instead, she crouched and petted Max again, making much of him in a way that made Anson feel a little lonely, truth be told. She hadn't tried to hug him, though, to be fair, her arms were so padded it didn't look like she could put them all the way down. Wrapping them around anything bigger than Max would be a feat.

"Elle?" he prompted, when she'd avoided looking at him for long enough that it became apparent she was procrastinating. "Did you think that me finding you here would help or something?"

"Did it?"

"My mom is still gone. Max can be distracted and move on from a…really awful experience by giving him a win…but…"

"But you're smarter than that," she said, squeezing the dog one more time and then standing up. "When I devised this plan I pictured you crawling inside, finding your toy…and I hoped it might help you."

"My toy?"

"The army man your mom used as a puppet to act out stories for you."

He'd never told her it was an army man. "Did you find…? Was the toy in there?"

She smiled and unzipped her crazy snowsuit, reached inside and pulled out his army hero action figure. Something in his gut twisted as she held the toy out to him and he felt the light plastic weight of it in his hand for the first time in twenty-five years.

"Sargent Stan." He said the toy's name and then stepped back to a bank of snow and sat, not feeling like his legs could support him suddenly. "Why would you even think to do this?"

She followed and knelt before him, pulled off her dirty mittens and stuffed them into the open monstrosity she wore so she could clean Sgt. Stan's face with her fingernail. "I know you already know what I'm going to tell you, but I think you still need to hear it."

He looked up from the doll at those warm brown eyes and nodded, not trusting himself to speak.

"You can't find something on the mountain that you didn't lose on the mountain."

It was like talking to her in the first hours they'd met. He knew she was saying something that she felt was important, but he needed some landmarks to try and run this linguistic obstacle course. He nodded, slowly, hoping she'd elaborate.

"I internet-stalked you."

He nodded again, still waiting.

"Your mom was an emergency room doctor."

"Yes." He could understand that statement.

"And so are you."

He nodded.

She added, "And you save people from the fate that befell her when she...saved you."

Max sensed his growing discomfort and came to sniff at his face. Anson leaned back and gently shoved the dog's head to his lap to pet.

Ellory added, "You lost her on the mountain. But you didn't. She died here, but she was found, and because she was found, you were found. She had a funeral."

All he could do was nod.

"She's not here, Anson. Because you didn't lose her on the mountain. Not really. But Sargent Stan..." She repeated the toy's name and then laid her hand on Max's head to pet him too. "You did lose him here. And now you have him back, and the memory of your mom doing whatever she could to make you feel better..."

Her voice strangled at the end and she looked away long enough to swipe her cheeks. When she looked back he saw her tears had streaked the dirt and muddied her up a little. Any other woman he knew would stop and clean her face at this point, but Ellory didn't and he suddenly knew why: dirt was natural. Like the material of her insane out-fit. Natural and real, like she was.

"I went there to find that because I feel like he's your totem. And because I really do think that Max needed to find someone..."

"He did." Anson murmured, not sure how he felt about all this. Or what she meant by totem, but all he could see was his mother's hand holding Sgt. Stan. He wished he could remember what she'd said...

"I found something else. Something I didn't expect. You didn't tell me..."

She slipped one hand into her pocket and when she pulled it out it was closed around something.

"I told you the whole story...all that I know, at least." He kept his eyes off the toy, it was too emotionally charged and he was barely keeping himself together. And he was afraid to look at whatever was in her hand.

"Then it's another piece to cobble together," she whispered, and opened her hand and held it out to him.

Dirt-covered and tarnished, his mother's locket rested in her little hand.

He couldn't move. And when he didn't reach

out for it Ellory popped the thing open with her fingernail and showed him the portrait he knew was inside: the one of him and Mom when he'd been a spaghetti-sauce-covered monster toddler, and she'd pressed her cheek to his for a close-up picture all the same. All smiles.

"You have her eyes."

He nodded, and swallowed, finally reaching for the piece of jewelry.

"She left her totem to protect you. Before she left. The rescuers probably just didn't see it." She paused and then added, "You can't control what other people do, that's what I learned from this Jude mess. You can't control anyone but yourself—whether they do something awful like Jude, or whether they're true heroes like your mom. All you can control is how you respond. I get why you're a doctor and why you and Max risk your lives for others." She stood and backed away from him, focusing on getting her dirty mittens back on, so he almost missed it when she whispered, "She'd be proud of you."

His mother would be proud of him, something he had heard from other people in his life, but had never believed. But when Ellory said it…he did believe it. And he suddenly wished he had something he could say to her that would help. He'd been so focused on Jude and Chelsea, on how the search had made him feel, he had neglected tending her in the way she tended him… She was still hurting. He'd done nothing to diminish it.

"I wouldn't try to clean it too much," she said, breaking through his thoughts. "The picture is fragile, and any chemicals that would remove the tarnish would probably ruin the photo. Plus…"

"Dirt is natural?" he asked, teasing a little.

"It is, but I was going to say…maybe there's still a trace of her. Even a particle. Maybe even protected by the tarnish." And then she shrugged, and turned toward the tree line and slogged off through the snow. "Which is also natural. Tarnish… Or you could ignore me."

"Doubtful." He closed the locket, unzipped his suit and stashed the precious cargo in an interior pocket. "Where are you going?" He zipped back up and stood to follow her.

"Lodge." She reached the trees and turned up the hill, using them like posts to help pull herself up through the snow. "It's cold."

And she was wearing the world's most ridiculous snowsuit. "Is it wet?" he asked, hurrying to catch up to her so he could link elbows and they could pull up the steep slope together.

"Yep. It doesn't hold water out as well as..." She looked at his face and stopped speaking, probably noticing how displeased he was with this little tidbit. Out in the cold, freezing for his benefit...

He let the silence go on between them for a few minutes before asking, "Are your feet cold?"

"My feet are fairly warm. Not wet, three pairs of wool socks. Boots two sizes too big."

When they'd made it far enough up the slope to reach the snowmobiles, she pulled away from him and climbed on hers. She waved a mittened hand at him and called, "Take care of yourself and Max," then turned around and zoomed across the slope, heading back for the lodge and leaving Anson to try and catch his breath.

His chest ached, though not from exertion or even from his cracked ribs.

Her farewell had sounded an awful lot like goodbye.

CHAPTER FOURTEEN

"She left."

Anson stood in the doorway of Miranda Dupris's office, staring at the woman. "What do you mean, she left?"

"I mean she isn't here any more. She doesn't work at the lodge any more. I told her we'd be happy to have her here for the whole year, guests don't just get hurt when skiing, but you and I both know that as much as she loved being here, she has her code and that code requires space." She paused and looked at him. "As well as no central heating. She's been making small changes, but she's still very against central heating."

Okay, so it had taken him a couple of weeks to figure his life out, what he wanted versus what he did. But he hadn't expected her to run away in the meantime. Winter wasn't even over yet. "Did she go back to Peru?"

She could be anywhere!

Mira shook her head.

"Do you know how to contact her?"

"Of course I do."

Best friend, guardian at the gate, torturing the guy who'd hurt her best friend. Right. He deserved that. "Will you call her, please?" He tried some honey, because what he really wanted to do was hose the woman down in vinegar. And shake her.

"What do you want to say to her?"

Definitely shake her. Except if he was going to be part of Ellory's life, he couldn't go shaking her best friend. And they obviously stuck together. Tight.

"I don't need to be vetted before you'll let me talk to her. Trust me."

"You hurt her," Mira said, and then sat down at her desk, hands linked as she fixed him with an unrelenting stare.

Anson sighed, closed the door and went to sit down.

If he had to jump through hoops to reach Ellory, it was his own damned fault. "I did."

"You don't understand, you made her break her resolution and then you hurt her on top of that."

"I understand. Believe me." He had to say something to convince her. "I don't know if she will want to take me back, but I have to talk to her even if it's just to tell her one thing. And if I have to go all the way to Patagonia to do it, I will go all the way to Patagonia."

Mira said nothing, just watched him.

"I love her, Mira."

"Is that what you want to say?"

"That, and I want to tell her something about her father."

She sat up straighter, brows surging to her hairline. "Did you go see him?"

"Yes, I did," Anson answered, then frowned, "After I told him what I'd come to tell him, he refused to tell me where she was. I didn't expect him to know, I just wanted to highlight this fact in a completely obnoxious manner."

An hour later, after he'd relayed a blow-by-blow account of his meeting with Ellory's parents, Anson left with a Main Street address in hand and the urge to shake Mira again.

He'd spent the whole time thinking Ellory had left the country, and she was just in town.

* * *

A brass bell at the top of the main door rang and Ellory popped her head round the corner from the back room. "We're not open for business yet," she called, but all other words died in her throat. Anson stood in the doorway wearing actual clothes, nothing orange in sight.

Jeans that fit his muscled frame well. A worn leather jacket hung open, revealing a flannel button-down over a navy thermal top.

He'd shaved.

His hair was combed back and not hidden beneath a knit cap.

And he had a plant with him.

Max, his perpetual companion, didn't stand on ceremony and obviously didn't feel any of the awkwardness the humans felt. He danced around the counter in that happy wagging-tail way of his to greet her.

Ellory greeted Max before he destroyed the place with his big swinging tail.

"Max," Anson grunted, "You're stealing the show, buddy. Go lie down." He snapped his fingers and pointed to the fire, which was enough. The big black Newfoundland all but pranced over and flopped onto the old worn wood floor of the building Ellory had leased from Mira.

Her heart in her throat, Ellory looked back at the man, and only then realized she should say something. "Thank you. For the…the…spa-warming gift."

"I wanted to get flowers but apparently you can't buy flowers that are locally sourced in winter." He approached the counter and thrust the potted fern at her.

She took the pot, careful not to accidentally touch the man, and set it on the counter. "It's really nice. Reminds me of the rainforest. Besides, cut flowers just die anyway. Nice of you to bring it by."

"I actually don't have any clue if the plant is a viable substitute… You're supposed to bring flowers when you apologize to the woman you love."

No preamble. He just laid it out there so boldly that her mind went blank.

"You can't control what other people do, right? That's what you said. You can't control what other people do…or think or anything. Just you, how you react."

"Right," she whispered, her hands starting to shake. The blasted bracelets jangled, and he noticed.

Before she could hide her hands, Anson reached out and took both of them, his thumbs on top to stroke the backs of her hands. "I visited your father."

"Oh, no… Did you hit him?"

"No. I wanted to, but he's a miserable old cuss, and nothing I can do will ever change that." He said the words slowly, like she hadn't already come to that conclusion on the mountain.

"I know that now. And I hate to say it, but Jude taught me that lesson."

He nodded, seeking her gaze and holding it for the space of several heartbeats. She loved his eyes…

"That's why you left us? So I could figure everything out? It wasn't because you stopped loving us?"

Us. She knew he meant him and Max, not the two of them as a couple, but it was still cute how he was hiding in language a little bit.

"I never said I loved you." Having her hands in his gave her the confidence to torment him a little. It had been at least twelve years since she'd seen him on the mountain…a couple of weeks ago. Twelve really long years.

"Yes, you did."

"No, I didn't. I definitely never said that."

He shook his head, looking at her like she was crazy. "You did too."

"I never ever said that to anyone but my parents and Mira. Never. Not once."

"Well, I heard you say it." He let go of her hands suddenly and reached across the counter, his hands folding over her shoulders to pull her toward him as he leaned in to meet her. No working up to it, no flirting and coyness, he just kissed her like a starving man, like it was all he could do to keep from dragging her across the counter into his arms.

She did it for him. Ellory's arms stole around his shoulders and she hooked one knee on the counter to climb over. Warm hands slid to her waist and he helped drag her to the front with him, and right onto the floor, only deepening the kiss when he got her well and truly plastered against him.

By the time he came up for air the worried look

she'd seen in his eyes was gone, and he smiled. "And there you said it again."

"Did not." She grabbed his head and pulled him back down, not caring at all whoever happened to walk by the big glass windows on the old general store she was converting, and that they might see them making out.

Though she was really glad that she'd taken several days to clean and restore the hardwood floors with lemons and beeswax. Which reminded her... kissing and making out hadn't been their problem. They were really good at that.

"Say it," he grumbled. "I know you love me. You might as well admit it."

Ellory sighed and then nodded. "I love you. But that doesn't mean we're compatible."

He snorted softly. "Are you and Mira compatible?"

"Of course we are."

"You're totally different. And you still fit together. You and I? We're not that different, and we fit together. I can prove it."

"You cannot prove it."

"Things you'd do to improve the house and property—greenhouse, doghouse, solar panels everywhere, and a thermal well into the earth to get the heat without a drop of carbon in the atmosphere. How am I doing?"

She laughed up at him. "Proud that you figured that out? It's pretty obvious."

"I'm a smart guy, what can I say?"

"I can't really tell you if I like your little house or not. You never let me inside, smart guy."

"Okay, yes, I have made some mistakes. But you will love it, as much as you love me and Max."

"But I still never said that."

"Everything about you says it. Mira said you moved out of the lodge. Where are you living?"

She pointed up at the ceiling.

"Above the shop?"

A nod. "Spa."

"Is it furnished?"

"Mmm it has a futon…and a fridge. And a pot-bellied stove."

Because she hated central heating.

"What made you decide to stay?"

"What I realized in your cave." She started to look a little nervous then, and chewed her lip which made him want to kiss her some more.

"About my mom?"

"Sort of." She started wriggling to get out from under him, but Anson knew better than to let her get away again.

"Look at me. I just told you I love you. What can you possibly be afraid of?"

"You don't know how successful I've been with wrangling my compulsions."

"Tell me."

"I'm about half as obnoxious as I was." Ellory said, shrugging. "It's not going to happen overnight, and I don't want to just become whatever you want me to be. I want to be what I want to be, and I need some time to figure that out."

"Okay. If you want to wait, I can wait." He leaned down and brushed his lips against hers. "So is this a grocery?"

"Do you see fresh fruit? It's a spa, maybe a wellness center. There will be some natural remedies available, oils and decoctions for different common ailments—like muscle soreness, and the respiratory flush we used on our patient guests. And some other natural stuff. Like deodorants without propylene glycol and other bad chemicals. Meditation, yoga, and primarily treatments."

"Treatments?"

"Massage therapy…remember? And with Mira's old contacts there are a few serious ski competitors who will likely be bringing their physio orders here."

"How have the epiphanies affected your stance on children?"

She opened her mouth to say something and then shut it again, her shoulders creeping up.

"You don't know?"

"I didn't want to think about it," she confirmed, though with less energy than she'd spoken with up to that point.

It was better than her saying outright she wasn't allowed to have them because she wasn't supposed to be alive to breed a bunch of new people into existence. "Afraid it's too far off your new paradigm?"

"New paradigm?" she repeated, and then shook her head. "No. More afraid I might turn mean, like my father. What if my child, no matter how well I try to raise it, turns into the world's biggest polluter and consumer?"

"We won't let that happen." He'd slipped that "we" casually in there and watched her smile return before adding, "So long as you don't make them wear that snowsuit."

"You haven't asked me to marry you yet." She laughed, getting Max's attention.

Anson shoved the big furball back before they both got licked on the mouth. "I'm working up to it!" When Max would not be dissuaded from licking them, Anson stood and pulled her up from the floor, then set her on the counter where he could kiss her safely and add, "But, it's going to be a lot easier to ask now that you've already said yes."

She laughed against his lips. "I did not!"

"Yes, you did. I heard you. Plain as day."

Flinging her arms around his neck, she kissed him again and then peeked around him toward the entrance. "We have to lock the door. Because it's definitely time I give you the tour of my futon." With a bounce in her step she scampered to the door and then back to take him by the hand. "Just so you know, it's a naked futon tour. We like to keep things natural around here…"

EPILOGUE

"NO CHAMPAGNE."

Ellory Graves drank once a year. Once! But not this year. She looked at her new husband, who had spoken the words, and made a face at him as he shooed off the waiter carrying a tray laden with sparkling flutes of bubbling liquid amber yum-yum. They'd been married since Thanksgiving. True to his word, he'd waited until she was ready for the ring, which happened to be a few months after she'd been ready to make a baby…

"I brought a sparkling apple cider."

He flagged down another waiter, leaving Ellory to slowly spin on her bar stool, hand resting on her rounding belly that had finally reached the point where none of her shirts seemed long enough.

Mira was a few months further along than she was. Ellory had decided she could have one baby and not ruin the planet. And since every child needs a sibling…and Mira was making a baby…

"I'm almost afraid to make any resolutions this year," Mira said. "Like nothing can live up to the last year, so stop making them while we're ahead!"

"No way. We need a goal. I need a goal. Can we hold the resolution to midway through the year when the babies are out and we need to lose weight? Because you're looking mighty round, Mirry."

Jack stepped around his wife and laid a hand protectively on her belly. "Don't listen to her. You're perfect."

"Shut it, Sex Machine. I am trying to get out of doing work for the first half of the year!" Ellory laughed, leaning against Anson. It still felt surreal to her—the most negative and contrary resolutions they'd ever made had turned into blessings bigger than either could have imagined.

The universe really had a wicked sense of humor.

Although, if making negative resolutions was the way to ensure big changes in your life, she was done with that. Her life was perfect. No changes welcome!

"I'm going to learn how to turn flax into linen,"

Ellory said, snagging the sparkling cider and waiting for Mira to lift her glass. Nice and innocuous.

The countdown had started. She felt pressure on her back, spinning her stool so she faced him. "Leave the lady alone," Anson said, his lips right at her ear. "She's got her first New Year's kiss with her husband to attend to." He waited a beat, tilting his head to catch her eye, then added, *"Hint."*

He regularly made her laugh, and she knew their child's life would be full of love and laughter. Neither of them would allow anything into their lives that threatened that contented bubble of happiness they'd wrapped around their home.

Graves wasn't even a bad last name in the right context. A love they'd both go to their graves to protect? Good context, and Anson had the perfect example of it.

When the crowd hit one, he swooped in and delivered a kiss full of promise and acceptance. Her favorite pastime.

And it was even good for the environment.

* * * * *

MILLS & BOON®
Large Print Medical

August

A DATE WITH HER VALENTINE DOC	Melanie Milburne
IT HAPPENED IN PARIS...	Robin Gianna
THE SHEIKH DOCTOR'S BRIDE	Meredith Webber
TEMPTATION IN PARADISE	Joanna Neil
A BABY TO HEAL THEIR HEARTS	Kate Hardy
THE SURGEON'S BABY SECRET	Amber McKenzie

September

BABY TWINS TO BIND THEM	Carol Marinelli
THE FIREFIGHTER TO HEAL HER HEART	Annie O'Neil
TORTURED BY HER TOUCH	Dianne Drake
IT HAPPENED IN VEGAS	Amy Ruttan
THE FAMILY SHE NEEDS	Sue MacKay
A FATHER FOR POPPY	Abigail Gordon

October

JUST ONE NIGHT?	Carol Marinelli
MEANT-TO-BE FAMILY	Marion Lennox
THE SOLDIER SHE COULD NEVER FORGET	Tina Beckett
THE DOCTOR'S REDEMPTION	Susan Carlisle
WANTED: PARENTS FOR A BABY!	Laura Iding
HIS PERFECT BRIDE?	Louisa Heaton

MILLS & BOON®
Large Print Medical

November

ALWAYS THE MIDWIFE	Alison Roberts
MIDWIFE'S BABY BUMP	Susanne Hampton
A KISS TO MELT HER HEART	Emily Forbes
TEMPTED BY HER ITALIAN SURGEON	Louisa George
DARING TO DATE HER EX	Annie Claydon
THE ONE MAN TO HEAL HER	Meredith Webber

December

MIDWIFE...TO MUM!	Sue MacKay
HIS BEST FRIEND'S BABY	Susan Carlisle
ITALIAN SURGEON TO THE STARS	Melanie Milburne
HER GREEK DOCTOR'S PROPOSAL	Robin Gianna
NEW YORK DOC TO BLUSHING BRIDE	Janice Lynn
STILL MARRIED TO HER EX!	Lucy Clark

January

UNLOCKING HER SURGEON'S HEART	Fiona Lowe
HER PLAYBOY'S SECRET	Tina Beckett
THE DOCTOR SHE LEFT BEHIND	Scarlet Wilson
TAMING HER NAVY DOC	Amy Ruttan
A PROMISE...TO A PROPOSAL?	Kate Hardy
HER FAMILY FOR KEEPS	Molly Evans